J   Myers, Anna.
         Graveyard girl.

$14.95

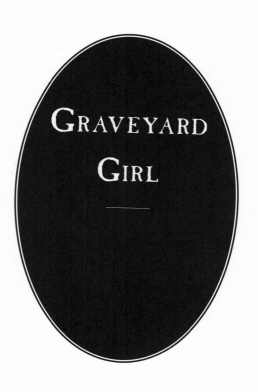

GRAVEYARD
GIRL

ALSO BY ANNA MYERS

Red-Dirt Jessie

Rosie's Tiger

GRAVEYARD GIRL

ANNA MYERS

WALKER AND COMPANY

New York

First published in the United States of America in 1995 by Walker
Publishing Company, Inc.

Published simultaneously in Canada by Thomas Allen & Son Canada,
Limited, Markham, Ontario

Library of Congress Cataloging-in-Publication Data
Myers, Anna.
Graveyard girl / Anna Myers.
p.   cm.
Summary: During the yellow fever epidemic in Memphis in 1878,
twelve-year-old Eli and Addie, a young child he befriends, struggle
to survive with the help of Addie's ghost-mother and a girl who
works at the busy graveyard.
ISBN 0-8027-8260-4
1. Yellow fever—Tennessee—Memphis—History—19th century—
Juvenile fiction. [1. Yellow fever—Tennessee—Memphis—
History—19th century—Fiction. 2. Memphis (Tenn.)—History—
Fiction. 3. Ghosts—Fiction.] I. Title.
PZ7.M9814Gr   1995
[Fic]—dc20   95-1770
CIP   AC

Book design by Jennifer Ann Daddio

Printed in the United States of America

2   4   6   8   10   9   7   5   3   1

For my children, Ginny Elizabeth, Benjamin Paul,
and Anna-Maria, of whom I am very proud,
and who as young adults
are beginning to make lives away from home.

The Lord watch between me and thee, when we
are absent one from another.
Genesis 31:49b

Acknowledgments

For help with research, I appreciate the work of Catherine Evans, who shared material from the Mississippi Valley Collection at the University of Memphis, and the staff of the Memphis Room at Memphis/Shelby County Public Library.

As always I also relied heavily on the support of my family, especially the Memphis branch, Shirley and Charles Biggers, and of course my husband, Paul Myers.

GRAVEYARD

GIRL

Memphis
Daily Appeal

August 8, 1878

The City is prostrate with sickness and grief. The air is thick with poisons. It seems everyone remaining in Memphis is doomed to become a victim.

September 9, 1878

Dr. R. W. Mitchell estimates that more than 3,000 Memphians are suffering from the yellow fever.

Residents near Elmwood Cemetery who have complained that bodies have been left unburied there overnight were reminded yesterday that all laborers leave the grounds at 6, consequently all bodies brought to the graveyard after that hour must remain unburied till the next day.

One

THE FEVER STRUCK THE POOR FIRST, REACHING OUT along the river to chill the people in the shanties of Pinchgut and Boxtown. Victims lay shaking with cold, then burning with body heat and retching violently. Next the dreaded yellow color crept across them. The crisis came after seven hours. The fever went down. If it came again, a coffin was ordered. No time could be wasted, because coffins were hard to come by in Memphis during the summer of 1878.

Eli Mahoney sat beside his mother's bed. While his father walked the floors, it was Eli who put the yellow cardboard fever signal out on the door. It was Eli who covered his mother with three quilts, all there were in the house. It was Eli who mopped her face and arms with water when the fire raged inside her. It was Eli who wiped away the vomit. It was Eli who closed his mother's eyes for the last time for her and who put out the black cardboard beside the yellow to show that a coffin was needed.

Eli listened for the sounds of his father's grief. Thomas Mahoney was not a quiet man, and Eli expected him to wail out his sorrow, to beat the thin walls until the dishes in the cupboard rattled. But his father, ignoring Eli completely, just settled himself quietly in a corner.

In the next room the son had no time to wonder at the father's behavior. Molly also had the fever, and it was Eli who tended his little sister.

Finally he heard footsteps behind him. "She'll not make it," said Thomas from where he leaned against the doorway.

So unfamiliar was the tone of his father's voice that Eli turned to look, checking to make sure that it was indeed Thomas who spoke.

"The child will die, I tell you."

The cold words of this stranger father chilled the boy, and he shifted his attention back to the small form on the cot. "Live, Dumplin'," he whispered, and he smoothed back the red curls from her damp forehead. "Please try now, Dumplin'. Try to live."

Molly made no response, and Eli leaned near her face. She could hear him. Eli was sure of that. Five years it had been since his own bout with the cursed fever, but he remembered still his mother's voice calling to him through the thick, suffocating fuzziness that had seemed to clutch him.

"Hold on to me." He squeezed Molly's hot hand, afraid that if he turned it loose, death would come to steal away the small body.

"Wasting ye breath, lad." Thomas moved over to the window. "Death is everywhere, it is, just like when I was of your size in the old country. Me ma, me da, me brothers all dead. I come across the ocean, I did, but death's tracked us down."

Eli clenched his teeth. He had never heard his father talk of tragedy before, but it was Molly he had to think of now. "She might live. Me and you, we both lived."

"We did that." Thomas's voice was low and remote. "We beat death off that time, but the yellow jack wasn't so fierce in seventy-three." He pointed toward the window. "Look out there, lad. No one stirring on the street, not even a boat on the river. Half the city's fled. What's left is either acclimated like you and me or bound to die."

"Hush!" The boy waved his father away. "She'll hear you."

The man ignored Eli's words. "No food, not even milk for the wee ones, and me mother too weak even to cry." His voice had an eerie sound to it, and he began to pace again. "One dead, now two."

Eli was not sure whether his father was referring to his childhood or to the present, but he was desperate to stop the strange voice.

He let go of Molly's hand to go to his father, but Thomas ignored Eli and kept moving back and forth across the worn floor. "Ma's grave," Eli blurted out. "Shouldn't you see to Ma's burying?"

Thomas stopped walking and stared at his son as if his presence were a surprise. "Buryin'. Yes. A cemetery, but no pauper's grave." He shook his large head. "I won't have me Ruthie in a pauper's grave. She'll be buried in the churchyard, laid away by a holy father, all proper." He turned to Eli. "But money, lad. They'll want money."

Eli was stunned. "There's money in her sewing box, money she was saving." He reached out and laid his hand on his father's sun-freckled arm. "But Da. You know Ma can't be buried by the church." Eli wanted to shout. How could his father have forgotten? "Elmwood, Da. You could arrange for Ma at Elmwood. She's a Methodist, not a Catholic. Remember? You either, hardly. Not going to mass in so long."

Molly groaned and began to thrash on her bed. Eli left his father and went back to take up the small hand again.

"Not Catholic, you say?" Thomas sank, bewildered, on to a chair and leaned his head on the kitchen table. "I was Catholic then." The strange faraway tone was back in Thomas's voice, and Eli shivered as he listened. "Potatoes rotten in the field, no food, not even enough to keep me wee brothers alive. I lived, though. For no reason me breath kept right on comin'. Wantin' to die, all the while. Never carin', for truth, to live until I come across Ruthie."

Eli was shocked. His huge father, full of life, full of laughter and rough jokes with the men on the docks. His father, a singer of songs and a teller of stories, his father had wanted to die in Ireland. Hadn't all of Thomas's talk of the old country been packed with green fields and laughing children? And the songs, the ones Thomas had taught Eli as they fished, hadn't they been Irish songs overflowing with love for Irish sod?

There was no time to ponder. Molly's face was as red as live coals. Eli wiped at it with the wet cloth, but he had to say something more. "Da, you never said. You never said at all. You never told me how it was."

Thomas rose and backed toward the door. "A man's not apt to draw from Hell when he's spinning yarns for the young." He waved his hand to take in the child on the bed. "Ye won't talk easy of this." He glanced over his shoulder at the door. "I can't stay here. Dead bodies all in a row."

Molly groaned, and Eli forced a spoon full of water between her dry lips. There was no time to worry about his father. Shouldn't it be the other way? Shouldn't his father be worried about Molly and about him? "See to the burying," he said, but he felt strange, giving his father instructions.

Eli had work to do. The Howard Association nurse had half promised to come back today, but she would not enter unless he put a new supply of carbolic acid in the saucers placed around the sickroom in an effort to fight the germs.

Reluctantly, he left Molly's side and began to spoon the clear liquid from the jar the nurse had given him. He worked quickly, knowing he would smell the nurse even before she entered the open door. Miss Tyler, like many of the other Howard Association workers, puffed on a cigar when she was near a patient. "Made me gag at first," she had confided to Eli on her last visit. "Still hate the thing, but some claim the smoke's a shield against the poison."

The smell of the fresh acid burned Eli's nose and made his eyes water, but he filled four saucers. When the work was done, he settled again beside his sister. "The nurse'll come," he whispered. "Nurse Tyler will come. She'll make you feel better."

Time passed with no sound except Molly's labored breathing and pitiful moans. Eli knew his father would be gone for quite a spell. Elmwood Cemetery was a good distance away. The wagon had taken his mother's coffin, but his father would have trouble finding transportation on the deserted streets. He tried to wait patiently for the nurse, but every time Molly pulled in her breath he feared she might not let it out again. Just when he thought he could bear the quiet no longer, he heard a step near the door.

"She's here," he told Molly, and he jumped up to check the saucers on the table, anxious to make sure the acid had not evaporated, but it was Thomas who appeared.

Without a word he crossed to the table and laid down a piece of paper. "Receipt from Elmwood Cemetery. Two places, two graves, paid for."

"No," Eli shouted. "Molly won't die. The nurse will come. She'll have something to make Molly better."

Thomas did not seem to hear. "Elmwood's a fair piece of green. Two graves all paid for and an angel of a girl to say a prayer."

Eli reached out toward his father. For a second he considered grabbing the man, shaking some sense into him, but his father moved back, and the boy let his arms drop back to his sides. "Did you not hear me?" he shouted. "Molly don't need a grave. She don't." He motioned wildly. "Come over here, Da. Come and touch her face. It's our little Molly, and she's going to live. She's got to."

Thomas held up his hand as if to keep the boy away. "It's sorry I am, lad. Me strength is gone.

Can't watch the dying, can't stand this wailin' city." He shook his head. "A better man than me ye are, Son. Ye will see to Molly, and the day might come ye can understand ye Da." He turned, and without looking back, he left the house.

For a moment Eli was too stunned to move. This was not his father. By the time he ran to the door, Thomas was several feet away. "Da!" he screamed. "Da, where you headed? Da, come back. I need you." Thomas kept walking.

Eli held on to the door frame to steady himself. Well, let him go, he thought. Likely he would wander off down by the river looking for rabbit tobacco for his pipe.

Eli did not want his father in the house while Nurse Tyler visited anyway. There should be no talk of Molly's grave. Miss Tyler was busy, if she thought there was no chance for Molly, she might not even stay.

His father would feel better after a walk by the river. Da loved the river. It would be hard for Da, Eli thought, without Ma. It would be hard for Eli too, but they would hold up. There was Molly to consider.

He went back to the bedside. Finally, the nurse did come, blowing cigar smoke but having no hope to share. "There's little to do, I'm afraid." Her tired face looked sad. "Some are trying the leeches, bleeding the poor souls, but I've never seen it help."

"No." Eli shook his head. "Molly would hate that. Crawly things fret her so."

Miss Tyler gave the girl a quick sponge bath and forced castor oil into the lifeless mouth. "It's all there is." She reached for her bag but lingered near the door. Eli felt there was something she wanted to say. She's going to tell me that Molly will die, he thought, and he waited, dreading the words.

The nurse leaned around the boy to peer into the cook room. "Your father about? I thought I saw him." She paused, embarrassed. "Some man like him, I guess, climbing up onto the top of the train down at the Main Street depot when it paused to throw off mail. Surely, I was mistaken."

Eli did not look at the nurse. With a terrible certainty he knew she was right. His father had sneaked onto the train to escape the dying. "You're alone," a voice in his head shrieked. "You're alone and Molly's going to die."

Miss Tyler was watching him. "Surely I was mistaken?" she repeated.

"Reckon so, ma'am." He kept his eyes down, and his cheeks burned with shame for his father. "It'd take a mighty sorry fellow to run out now. You was most surely mistaken."

The woman studied the boy's face for a mo-

ment more, nodded her head slowly, and said
only, "Bless your heart. I'll look back in directly."

After she was gone, Eli looked around the
quiet house and knew he was truly alone. Settling
again beside Molly, he held her hand and waited.
When the afternoon sun made the shadows of the
wharf pilings stretch farther out across the river,
Molly's labored breathing stopped, and when that
breathing stopped a great coldness came to Eli
despite the hot September air, a coldness as if the
mighty Mississippi itself had turned suddenly to
white ice, and he had stretched his body upon it.

After the coffin wagon had delivered one coffin, child-sized, Eli lifted his little sister's body to
place it among the mixture of tar and acid, put
into the box by the driver as an attempt to protect
the living. Now there was nothing left to do but
wait for the other wagon, the one with six great
horses that carried the dead to burial.

He made no move to burn the bedclothes or
the mattress. All day fires could be seen up and
down the streets of Memphis, and at night the
flames cast ghostly shadows on empty sidewalks.
But those people who had started the blazes had
someone left to protect.

Eli looked around him. His mother would
have fussed about the dirty dishes and the grits
spilled and dried on the stove. "Lands, it's a pig-

sty," she would have said. "It ain't decent, living like puredee hogs."

"It's OK, Ma," he whispered. "There's no one left to live here anyways. There ain't a living soul left, and that sure includes me."

He would go, he decided. When the dead wagon came, he would beg for a ride to the cemetery, see Molly buried, and then he would go. Quickly he gathered his other pair of pants and his best shirt. He was about to roll them together when his glance lingered on his mother's Bible. He added it to the bundle.

Eli settled himself then near the wooden box and waited for the wagon. At last it came. "Bring out your dead," the driver's voice echoed through the empty street. "Bring out your dead."

The coffin was made of light wood, but still it was hard for Eli to lift. He stumbled out of the doorway and almost dropped the box. "Wait now, youngun, and we'll give you a hand," called the large black man who was the driver, but Eli struggled on, not waiting for the two men who were climbing down to help.

"Sure enough strong for your size," the driver commented when he was down and taking one end of the coffin. He searched Eli's face. "Not sick, is you?"

"Acclimated."

"Lucky," commented the driver's assistant, and Eli whirled around to face him.

The remark had set off the anger raging inside the boy, and he made his hands into fists. "Lucky?" He threw the word back at the pale, thin young man. "Let's see am I lucky enough to whup you?"

"Whoah, now. There ain't no cause to get in a row with us." The black man laid a large hand on the boy's shoulder. "We ain't the cause of this devil yellow jack." There was a calmness in his voice, and Eli relaxed his hands.

The assistant cleared his throat and reached for a notebook from the wagon seat. "Name of the deceased?" Eli told them his little sister's name. "Only six," he added, but he looked down quickly, afraid of seeing sympathy in the strangers' eyes.

The young man wrote the name and placed a number on Molly's coffin. "You'd be requesting burial in the pauper section, I assume."

Eli stiffened again. "No, sirree, I sure ain't." He took the receipt from his pocket and shoved it toward the assistant, who offered Eli a nod of apology.

"Paid for, McLemore. Paid in advance," the young man said. Then he studied his paper for a second. "This makes twenty," he added. "Suppose we ought to knock off now?"

The older man looked up at the sun. "Be pushing to get these in the ground 'fore six. Graveyard Girl sure to fuss if we to bring in more than get put away."

"Can I ride along to the cemetery?" Eli said the words quickly, looking down as he spoke. There was no answer, and the boy, wondering if he had been heard, was forced to look up. Both men were studying him. "I'd powerful like to be there to see my little sister put away." It bothered Eli to plead.

"Well, now, I ain't allowed to carry along mourners." The driver shook his head.

Eli tightened his grip on the edge of Molly's box. "I'll work," he said. "Swear I will. I'll tote the coffins, do anything."

"Wouldn't be no real harm in carrying the boy with us, you figure? It being time for us to turn back to Elmwood anyways?" It was the assistant, and Eli was glad he hadn't fought the young man.

"Reckon not, and reckon I don't zackly always follow every little bitty rule." The driver smiled at Eli. "They calls me McLemore, and this here is Victor."

Eli put out a hand to each of them in turn. "My name's Eli," he said, "and I'm beholding to you. Right beholding." He settled himself on the sideboard near Molly's coffin.

Victor was climbing back up the seat and

called to Eli, "Wouldn't you care to ride up front with us?"

"Believe I'll stay here if it's just the same to you."

"Suit your own self, boy. Likely ain't hankering none after company, huh?" McLemore reached for the reins but twisted back to look at Eli. " 'Bout helping out, though. That'd be up to the Graveyard Girl."

"You don't work for the Howard Association, then?"

"Oh, the Howard fellows is the ones pay me all right, but it's sure enough the Graveyard Girl says what comes to pass in Elmwood Cemetery."

Just briefly Eli wondered who the Graveyard Girl was, but he didn't bother to ask. What did the goings-on in the cemetery matter to him? What did anything matter to him now? Again he shivered with the great inner coldness. He'd see Molly put away, make sure she rested beside their mother. Then, as soon as he could, he would leave Memphis.

The wagon was rolling now. Soon they would be out of Pinchgut. Eli looked at the shabby houses lining the street and at the ones down nearer the river, which were built up on stilts to avoid rising water. Here he had lived, always, within sight of the great stream, always in one hovel or another.

They were moving up out of the poorer area. But Eli could still see the Mississippi flowing peacefully, untouched by the city's troubles. No steamer pulled into the deserted docks, no skiffs floated along. No river songs joined the sound of the waves against the shores.

Eli closed his eyes, trying to force out the vision in his head, he and his father working side by side as roustabouts to unload a big steamship. "Begora! If it's not meself hard pressed to stay up with you, lad." Later, when the sun was about to go down, they would fish from their own raft, rolling with the rhythm of the river's easy laps, and always as they headed toward home there were Thomas's songs.

"I can do without you, river," Eli muttered. "I'm fixing to forget all about you and all about him."

He made his mind a blank then, allowing no thought to accompany the sound of the great wheels and the horseshoes, at first on the cobblestones of the river area and then on the great wooden planks of the city streets.

Elmwood was on the other side of the city, and Eli determined to do nothing but rest. The horse, not slowed by other traffic, moved at a good pace. Except for the terrible rotting animal and sewer smell when they crossed the Gayoso

Bayou, where Memphis dumped its filth, Eli enjoyed the breeze and the quiet.

When they reached Durion Avenue, the
wagon turned through the gate of the picket fence
surrounding Elmwood Cemetery. The bell forced
its way into Eli's thoughts before he saw the girl.
She was tall but slight of build. With each ring she
leaned her entire weight on the bell rope. "The
Graveyard Girl," McLemore called out from the
front of the wagon, and he pointed toward
the bell ringer.

Two

ELI STARED AT THE SLENDER GIRL BY WHOM Mc-
Lemore obviously set a good deal of store. Ain't
much older than me, he thought. Plain too. The
girl's face might have been pretty once. Now it
was too thin and tired looking, and the brown
hair framing the face was limp and lifeless. Not
impressed with Her Highness of the Cemetery, he
told himself, and leaned indifferently over the
wagon's edge to spit.

When the horses stopped, Eli jumped to the
ground and reached for Molly's coffin, but
McLemore turned on the seat and shook his great
head. "Leave the box," he said. "I needs be telling
her about you first." He motioned toward the girl.

"Who is this Graveyard Girl?" Eli asked as he
strained to match the big man's stride on the way
toward the bell tower.

"Grew up here, she did, in yonder cottage,

just her and her pappy. He be the sexton. But he
come down with the fever early on. By the time
the Howard fellers hired me, the daughter had
plumb took over his job. Name's Grace, but folks
is took up calling her the Graveyard Girl." He
stopped and laid a hand on Eli's shoulder. "She
ain't . . ." he paused, considering. "The Graveyard
Girl, she ain't . . . regular."

"Huh? Reckon I don't get your meaning."

"You will. Iffen you stay hereabouts, you sure
enough is bound to."

Eli shrugged his shoulders. "Seems peculiar,
letting a puny girl stay on trying to do a man's job
just on account of her father's dead."

McLemore laughed. "It's powerful plain you
ain't never made the acquaintance of Miss Grace. I
sure don't recollect ever hearing nobody call her
puny. Oh, and her pappy didn't pass. The fever
didn't taken him. Weak, though. Never leaves his
room. The Graveyard Girl does it all, sees to her
pappy, records the names of all the dead, hands
peace to the grieving, and rings that bell. Swears
not one body will go to a grave in Elmwood
without a bell sounding, even tolls for them that's
put in No Man's Land."

They were beside her now, but the Graveyard
Girl did not stop ringing the bell. Eli watched
skeptically. McLemore had claimed this girl
handed peace to the grieving. A bitter smile played

about his lips. That's a pretty tall order. He studied the lank girl. Let's just see you give a hunk of peace to Eli Mahoney, he thought.

The girl did not even glance in their direction. As she pulled the rope her face was expressionless, her body almost trancelike. "Mr. James Elder," she read from a list written in bold black letters lying near her feet, and her voice was clear and surprisingly strong, as clear and powerful as the bell.

"We'll have to wait till she's pure done." McLemore whispered and pointed to the list. Eli could see there was one more name.

"Mary Gatson."

Eli waited, thinking the girl would turn toward them then, but she didn't. "Now," she said, but she did not glance at the observers, and Eli knew she was not talking to them. "Now I will ring the bell for a soul not resting in Elmwood. He is being put away on another ground, but I ring for him because he was a true friend to Memphis. Father Joseph Fitzhugh."

Eli started at the name. Father Joseph had served the people of Pinchgut and had come by to pray for Eli's mother and Molly. Eli had liked the young priest, had been touched by his concern for a family whose only Catholic had not been to mass in years.

"Death comes, my son, but it need not separate us from those we love," Father Joseph had said to Eli after the prayer.

The boy had resisted. "But they might live." He pulled at the priest's frock. "Don't you think they might live?"

The young priest had wiped at his own feverish face. "There's always hope, lad. I pray they will, but this fever is strong." He dropped his gaze. "The truth is, I'm sick myself."

Eli had been shocked. "But you won't die, Father. Surely God will spare his holy men."

Eli remembered that Father Joseph had smiled. "Death comes for us all, lad. I've no fear of dying." His young face had become troubled then. "I only hope one of my own will be left alive to say the rites for me."

And now Eli stood listening to the Graveyard Girl sound the bell in Father Joseph's name. The bell rang out its death toll, and the boy studied the grass on the cemetery's gentle little hills. No tears came to his eyes for the young priest who had laughed with his father beside the river over stories from the old country. There was no pain inside, only empty coldness, and he was glad.

For a second he did consider bowing his head, but he kept his neck straight. Little good prayer had done him. He would leave it behind with his dead family. He watched a squirrel come down from a tree and run around a tombstone.

After the bell grew silent, the girl straightened her body and looked long into Eli's face.

McLemore fidgeted and cleared his throat. "This here lad rode along with me from down in Pinchgut." The man kept his eyes lowered and spoke hesitantly, the way, Eli thought, he would in the presence of a dignitary. "I figured wouldn't nobody fault me over much, my load not being anyways near as big as 'twas this morning. It's his little sister he's hankering to see put away." He reached out to pat Eli's back. "Says he'll work for the ride. 'Spect he'd be hungry too."

Eli drew himself away from McLemore's touch. He had no need of pats on the back or of charity meals. He felt uneasy, knowing the Graveyard Girl was watching him.

"How old are you?" she asked.

He opened his mouth ready to say, "Fourteen," but the girl's gray eyes seemed to look deep into his mind. "Twelve," he said, "but thirteen in a few months."

"Your family?"

"All dead from the fever." It wasn't a lie, he told himself. His father was as dead to him as his ma and Molly. But even so he could not look at the girl as he spoke.

"You could go out to one of the camps. They'd take you at Father Matthew's camp or even at Camp Williams."

Eli knew about the camps on the outside of town where people who feared the fever but did not have the money to go far away lived in tents. He was not interested in living in a group camp with crowds of people. He held up his chin. "Ain't needing to run. I'm acclimated, had the fever in seventy-three."

"They're taking orphans at Saint Mary's."

Eli bristled. Who was this almighty girl? Gouging him toward an asylum for babies! She couldn't hardly be called full growed neither. He made no attempt to hide his disgust. "You'll not find me at no orphans' asylum, me doing a man's work for now these three years. I'll be seeing to my own self altogether from here on out."

"What's your name?"

"Eli." He folded his arms across his chest and made no addition of his last name. He was definitely tired of this girl and her questions, but something stopped him from walking away.

"Well, Eli, there's work aplenty here. The Howard Association won't pay you. They don't hire on anyone your age, but if it's food you want, I cook for my father and there's extra. I've no room for you to sleep in, but"—she paused and waved her arm to survey the cemetery—"there's lots of room if you've no objection to sleeping among the dead. Not likely to get too airish, but if it should or in case of rain, there's the little chapel for shelter."

"Thank you." His words were stiff with no real trace of gratitude. "I'll be glad for a bite and a place to sleep. It's accustomed I've grown to the dead, but I'll only stay tonight. Moving on I'll be. Gone come morning. Think I'll head west." He gave his head a determined nod, pleased with the decision. "Yes, out West it is for me."

"How will you travel?"

Eli shrugged his shoulders. "No traffic on the river. Even the fishing skiffs won't pull in at the docks." He looked down, then found himself saying what he was thinking. "Besides, I won't go near the water again. I hate the river and them that work on it."

"I doubt you could get on a train, not to go any farther than the camps. Most towns won't accept travelers from Memphis."

He kicked at a rock and let the scowl loose to take over his face. "I've heard tell of folks sneaking onto train tops to hide when ain't nobody looking."

"So much anger." She looked directly into his eyes. "You need to work. Stay here and work. Working leaves no time for anger." She brushed her hand across her face. "And little time for tears."

"Tears ain't my problem. Eli Mahoney don't

cry." He jammed his hands hard into his pants pockets. He could feel her looking at him. He wished she were a boy. He would fight any boy who made him feel so uncomfortable.

"You don't cry, Eli Mahoney?" Her face suddenly looked very sad. "You don't cry. What a pity." She turned and walked away then. "I need the list," she called to Victor. "Any unknown bodies this time?"

Eli stood very still and watched the Graveyard Girl cross the grass. He wanted to dislike her, but there was something about her, something that beat against the wall he was working to build around himself.

Three

ELI HIMSELF HELPED MCLEMORE LIFT MOLLY'S BOX
from the great wagon. This is it, he thought, the
last thing I'll ever do for my little sister. It was, in
fact, he decided, the last thing he would ever do
for anyone other than himself. He was alone now,
would always be alone, would never want it any
other way again.

They lowered the small box down into the
hole beside his mother's mound. McLemore's end
bumped once against the newly spaded earth, and
Eli winced. "Easy now," he whispered, but he
was unsure as to whether he spoke to the man or
to Molly.

When he straightened up, the Graveyard Girl
was there, waiting.

"A prayer now," she said and bowed her head.
McLemore did too. No one spoke. They'll wait a

long time if it's me praying they're waiting for, Eli thought. He did not close his eyes.

After a moment the girl said, "Father, receive this young soul gently into your arms."

"I'll help with the others now," said Eli, and he turned away quickly as the digging crew came to cover the box with dirt.

Without thought or feeling, the boy's hands reached for the rough wooden boxes. Without thought or feeling, he helped carry those boxes to the waiting graves. Maybe I'm dead too, he reasoned, but his stomach rumbled out its cry for food. So, he told himself, you are alive. Must be, else hunger wouldn't be gnawing at your innards. You're alive all right, not that it's a blessing.

Most of the coffins, belonging to those who had either no one left to arrange burial or who had no money for the arrangement, were deposited in a great trench opened up in No Man's Land. There the boxes were laid end to end with no mark made for where one grave began and another ended. Still, every known name was recorded, and the bell sounded even for the unknown.

"The last ring will be for your Molly," the Graveyard Girl had told Eli. "I'll give it an extra hard ring for your little sister."

When it came, when he heard the great bell tolling for Molly, he knew it was really all over. He could feel McLemore studying him.

"Why not rest a bit? Wouldn't nobody fault you," the black man said, but Eli only shook his head. His insides felt as if they were made from iron like the funeral bell.

"Come to the cottage," the Graveyard Girl had told him. "There's sweet potato pie for your supper," and after the last box was deposited, his hunger pulled him toward her house.

At the open door of the cottage, he paused just a moment before knocking. Grace sat at a small table with a pen in her hand. Before her was a great black leather ledger, and she copied names from Victor's notebook onto the lined pages, making row after row of neat black letters.

She responded to his knock with, "Come in and get your plate from the cupboard." Her voice was welcoming, but she barely glanced up from her work. Eli, not anxious for company, would have taken his food outside to eat, but she motioned for him to sit at the other end of the table.

The only noises came from a dove cooing softly somewhere outside, and from the scratch of the girl's pen. Eli concentrated totally on filling the hollow of his stomach, but took no real pleasure in the sweet yellow food.

He had almost finished when she spoke. "I remember your father, Eli. You're a lot like him."

He put his spoon down hard against the plate. "No, miss. Begging your pardon, but I am not

like my da. Not one whit. I favor my mother and
her people down in Mississippi."

Her gaze seemed to see inside him. "Where is
your father, Eli?"

To his surprise, he found he wanted to tell her,
and it all came pouring out, the days of nursing
his mother and Molly, his father's strange behavior, Miss Tyler telling about the train. Finally, he
leaned back in his chair and said slowly, "He's a
sorry excuse for a man, my da is."

She nodded slowly and gave him a little half
smile. "Maybe. But then people do break. Who
can say what one of us might do if we live long
enough to see this fever done?"

Eli was embarrassed about spilling it all out
and was glad to shift the conversation to her. "But
you're acclimated, ain't you?"

She shook her head. "No."

"Why are you still here?"

"My papa needed someone to care for him.
Then, of course too, there are the names to record
and the bell to ring. Someone must bear witness.
Someone must," she paused, "must ring the bell."

He thought he understood. "Is it, then, that
you don't mind dying?"

"Oh, no. I want to live so much. I want to see
a wonderful deep frost come to wipe out this
fever and to see the people return to Memphis."
Excitement grew in her voice, and she stood up.

"I want to read in the *Appeal* how some doctor has learned the true cause of this yellow killer and how to prevent it." She leaned closer across the table. "I want to go back to my lessons at St. Mary's Episcopal School for Young Ladies."

She whirled around and went to a cupboard in the corner of the room. Bending down, she reached into a low shelf and came up with a bolt of shiny blue cloth, which she brought back to the table. "Look, see this. I bought it just before the fever started. My sewing's coming along nicely, the Sisters say. I bought this satin for our fall social." She unwound enough material to hold up to her shoulders. "What do you think, Eli? Does it suit me?"

For a second Eli forgot where they were. Grace was no longer the angel-like Graveyard Girl. She could have been any girl, and lately Eli had noticed that he fancied girls some, like Mazie, who worked in a kitchen where he sold fish and who tweaked Eli's cheek when she paid him. But then he came to himself. "Don't know nothing about party clothes," he muttered. "Ain't likely to be attending no parties."

Grace put down the material and sighed. "I'm sorry, Eli. Of course, your heart is broken now." She reached out and touched his hand ever so slightly. "But it will get better. It's bound to get better. Someday you'll feel like talking about parties." She smiled at him. "Someday there might even be a young lady in your life, and you might be asking me to teach you to dance."

"Ain't interested in dancing," he said, but he added, "You'll live though. I think you're bound to."

She had turned back to the cupboard, but before she put the satin away, she held it up for a second to catch the light from the lamp. "Oh, I hope so, Mr. Mahoney. I do hope so." Then her voice dropped, and she was more the girl he had first observed. "But if I die the world will go on. So many have died, and yet the grass still grows outside this door. Death is no stranger to me, Eli. I was born at Elmwood Cemetery."

There was something about this girl, some authority, some courage. She could talk, even now, of wanting to dance in a blue dress. A feeling stirred inside the boy. For a moment, he wavered. There were things he had wanted to do also. The thought frightened him, and he wanted to get away, wanted to crawl back into the deadness inside him. If he stayed dead, nothing could hurt.

He stood quickly and pushed the plate away from him. "I'm obliged for the food. I'll leave you to your work now."

He had almost made it to the door before she could respond. "Come back before you bed down.

I've an extra blanket will make a better bed than the grass."

Eli was glad to be outside. For a time he walked the paths between the trees. He paused and leaned against a great magnolia. The flowers were gone now, but the tree must have been full earlier. Eli's mother had loved magnolia blossoms. Sometimes in the spring he would swipe one from a low branch and carry it home. Ma would put it in a bowl, and the perfume would fill the air.

Without making a conscious decision to do so, he began to move toward the spot where his mother and sister rested. He stood looking down at the mounds. Suddenly exhaustion washed across him, and he dropped to the small strip between the graves.

If only his mother were there beside him instead of in the ground. He closed his eyes and saw her face, and words began to come quickly from his lips. "Where are you, Ma? Where is it you've gone to? I tried to take care of Molly, I did, but the fever beat us. I tried to hold on to her, like you always told me to do on the skiff. I wanted to hold on to her so bad, Ma. After you left us, I thought I could stand it somehow if I could just keep Molly with me."

He raised himself to a sitting position and shook his whole body as a wet dog might. "Quit it," he muttered. "You're carrying on for nothing." There was, he knew, no sense talking to Ma. She was gone.

He drew a deep breath and was about to force his weary body up when a hand touched his shoulder, making him start. The hand was small, and so was the voice that went with it. "Why don't you just cry?" Eli whirled about, half expecting to see Molly standing behind him.

"Crying's not bad. Go ahead and cry. My mother tells me crying washes out the hurt some." The little girl nodded her head to emphasize the wisdom of her words.

Eli stared at the girl. She could have been Molly's twin in size. Her eyes, like Molly's, were big and looked directly at him, interested in anything he might say or do. They were blue like his sister's too. The hair, though, was different. Molly's curls had been red and wild. This child had golden hair, obviously brushed often and tied back with a silk ribbon.

A great rush of anger came to Eli. It was unreasonable, he knew. Yet, he hated this child. He hated her eyes being like Molly's. He hated the way she looked at him, waiting. He hated that she stood here alive while Molly lay beneath the dirt. "What are you doing here?" He knew his voice was gruff, and he expected her to flinch or to look down.

But she stood her ground. "I heard you sound so sad. I'd like to make you feel better."

Anger made the boy clench his fists. "There's nothing the likes of you can do for me. Be off, now. You've no business wandering around these grounds."

She shook her head in disagreement. "Oh, but I do so have some business here. My mother said I should come. She said the Graveyard Girl would help me."

Eli looked toward the cottage, but there was no sight of Grace. "Likely she's seeing to her father now. Is your mother sick, then? If that's why you've come, you want to find a nurse. The Howard Association has doctors and nurses paid to help the sick. It's only the dead that comes for help to Elmwood."

She reached out and grasped the front of his shirt. "Please." Her voice broke, and she wiped with her free hand at her eyes. "Please, my mother said the Graveyard Girl would help me. She said, 'Go to the Graveyard Girl, Addie.' "

He pushed at her hand, but she clung to him. "Where is your mother?" He peered out toward the street. Maybe the woman was in a carriage, or perhaps a servant had driven the little girl to Elmwood. He'd say from the looks of her frilly pink dress and shiny black shoes that there was money for a servant. "Why are you and your mother still here in the city?" He did not try to prevent the sneer from forming on his lips. "Most of your kind packed up and ran weeks ago."

"Mama and Papa thought we were safe. I had the fever before when I was just a baby. Mama and Papa didn't get it even though they took care of me, so they thought we were all safe. Papa didn't want to leave his warehouse, but then he got sick. My father died, and then my mama got sick."

"Your mother is sick, then." Hadn't he just told her she needed a nurse? He pushed her hand loose from his shirt, but she grabbed at his pants legs. It was obvious he would have to do something to get rid of her. "I suppose I could go with you to the Peabody. The Howards have the nurses put up there in the hotel. Miss Tyler might be there, or we could leave word."

He started to move, but the child stood rooted and holding to his clothing. "Do you want me to help you find a nurse or not?"

"No need," she said. Her voice was very low, and Eli had to lean toward her to hear. "My mama died last week."

"Oh." He looked out over her head, unwilling to see her sorrow. "Well," he said, "there's been a lot of that, a lot of dying. Who's seeing to you now?"

"Sophie was. She took care of my mama

when she was just little, and she promised Mama
she wouldn't leave me until my aunt Elizabeth
came, but Sophie got sick too. She had to go
down to her sister's, and she said I must go to the
Peabody if she didn't come back."

Eli was agitated. "Well, girl, I'm still standing
here wondering what it is you want from the
Graveyard Girl."

"She will help me. We saw her here when my
papa was buried, and my mama said the Graveyard
Girl would help me."

"A week ago? You say your mother told you
that before she died last week? How did she expect
the Graveyard Girl to help?"

It was Addie's turn to show impatience. Her
lips formed into a pout. "Don't you understand
anything?"

Needs her behind busted, Eli thought. It's
spoiled this one is. Before he could say anything,
she went on. "My mama comes into my room
each night. Last night she came into my room,
and she spoke to me. 'Addie,' she said, 'go to the
Graveyard Girl. The Graveyard Girl will help
you.' "

Four

WHEN HE WAS SEVERAL FEET AWAY FROM THE CHILD, he stopped and looked back. She was as little as Molly, maybe even smaller. Standing there completely still with her head down, she looked like a statue, a small, sad statue. Eli had yelled at her, had told her to go away. But what if she had been Molly? What if he had died along with Ma and Molly had been left alone?

"All right," he shouted back to her. "I'll ask the Graveyard Girl if she's a mind to see you. You can wait there, I reckon."

The child clapped her hands as if she'd been given a present, and Eli turned away. The quick joy in her face wounded him. She's lost her folks, he thought, same as me, but she can make herself glad still. She's not gone all hard inside. He took big steps, glad to put distance between him and the girl.

He could see Grace through the open cottage door even before he reached the small stoop. The blue satin was spread on the table, and she was bent over it with scissors in her hand. " 'Cuse me, miss," he said as he knocked.

"Oh, Eli." Looking up at him, she blushed. "Do you think it's wrong of me to start to sew a party dress? I mean with all the heartbreak, all the mourning?"

He made no move to step into the cottage and its glow of lamplight. "I don't see as it's wrong to look forward to something if you can." He folded his arms across his chest. "But then I ain't what you call an expert on the subject."

Before she could reply, Eli went on. "There's a little girl out yonder." He motioned over his shoulder. "Daft she is, or else she's a big liar. Claims her dead mother came into her room and told her to come to you for help."

The Graveyard Girl dropped her scissors and rushed to the doorway. Eli moved aside slightly. "See. She's there by the gate."

"Poor little thing." Grace looked back at the cloth. "Probably I shouldn't be thinking of parties. I was wrong to take out the satin." She stepped back to the table. "I'll put this away and go to her."

Eli was surprised by the protest that half formed on his lips. What matter was it to him if this girl felt shamed over her interest in a party dress? He wanted to change the subject. "Did you hear what I said?" he questioned. "The little fool claims to be having talks with a dead woman."

"You think it can't be so?" She was folding the material, but she stopped and studied Eli.

From where he stood, he could see the spot where his mother lay. "No," he said. "It ain't possible." He wanted to add that if any soul could return, his mother would be beside him, would have been beside him when he had been forced, alone, to close his little sister's eyes for her. "Are you saying you do? You sure enough believe in ghosts?"

Grace sighed before she answered, and she did not look directly at Eli, more through him, beyond him. "I've lived my life on these grounds," she said, "and I've absorbed some things." She nodded her head. "There are souls that endure. They're still bound up in living because their work's not done. Yes, Eli, I believe they tarry."

Eli glanced again toward his mother's grave. Maybe the girl knew things he didn't. Maybe there was yet hope his mother might return, but he shook his head. He couldn't let himself hope, not anymore. "Nonsense!" he snorted.

The Graveyard Girl smiled. "Maybe," she said. "Maybe." She stepped past him out into the evening. "Let's see to the child. She needs our comfort."

Eli did not feel inclined to comfort anyone, but he did feel, for some reason, inclined to follow the Graveyard Girl. He was almost pulled, in fact, and he wondered why.

They did not have to walk far. Addie, who had been leaning dejectedly against the white picket fence, saw them. Coming to attention at once, she hesitated only briefly, then threw herself down the long brick walk, her blond curls bouncing.

The Graveyard Girl moved toward the little girl. Eli trudged behind.

"I knew you would come if I waited," Addie shouted. "I knew you would help me. Mama said you would. She said, 'The Graveyard Girl knows things.'" She was in Grace's arms, but she leaned around the bigger girl to look at Eli. "That awful boy said you were too busy." She stuck out her tongue. "He said Mama doesn't come to my room at night. Why did that awful boy say such things?"

Grace smoothed the child's yellow curls and made sympathetic shushing sounds. "That's Eli. Pay him no mind. Eli doesn't know very much, but he's a quick mind. I've no doubt he'll learn." Grace was looking up at him, grinning.

She's a sassy one, he thought, and Eli liked sassy girls. Before he caught himself, he almost grinned back, but then he remembered and whirled back toward the cottage. There was only one thing he really wanted to learn and that was how to get out of Memphis. For right now he would settle for getting away from these foolish females. "Think I'll . . ." He looked around until he spotted the well. "Think I'll go see about the water. Kitchen bucket was low."

"Wait." It was not a command. If it had been a command, Eli could have ignored the Graveyard Girl, but her words were a request. "Don't be mad. I shouldn't be teasing you now." She straightened up, but still held Addie's hand. "We need you, Eli. We surely do."

Get away from here, he told himself, but he made no move to leave.

The Graveyard Girl turned back to Addie. "Why did your mother send you here, honey? What is it that I can do to help you?"

"Mama didn't say." Addie's little face twisted with bewilderment. "I guess you're supposed to take care of me. Nobody's taking care of me." She choked back a sob. "I . . . I don't like to be all by myself."

"Of course you don't. Nobody wants to be all alone." The Graveyard Girl stroked Addie's hair. "We'll take care of you, won't we, Eli?"

The boy stiffened. Why was she dragging him into this? He'd better set them straight. "I ain't got nothing against being alone," he mumbled, but if they heard him, they paid no heed because when he turned and began walking back toward the cottage, they followed.

Addie, obviously glad to be near someone, half leaned on Grace as they walked. "I'm awful hungry," she said shyly. "But I guess it's not polite to ask for supper."

Grace gave her a quick hug. "You can ask Eli and me. You can ask for help anytime you need it."

Eli stared down at his badly worn boots and tried to think only about the evening sounds around him. He could not bear to remember the graves of his mother and sister or about his father, gone off on a train. Now he had to work too at blocking out thoughts of this Addie girl, little and alone. He would concentrate only on the crickets, which had begun their evening chirping.

"Where do you live?" Grace asked.

"I'll show you." Addie stopped walking, and she turned to Eli, so that he too could see her point off to her left. "Over there," she said. "My house is over there. See the big chimney."

Even in the twilight, he could see the top of a great white house with a huge brick chimney. "Carlile House?" Surprise made him forget that he did not want to be interested. "I know that place. I've sold fish at the back door to the cook."

"And I remember now too." The Graveyard Girl rubbed at her head. "Your father was one of the first not from the river hollow to come down with the fever. Before my father took sick, but I was here when the burial party came." She closed her eyes, remembering. "An especially pretty woman, sad yet very strong. I remember how she kept her arm on your shoulder while I rang the bell. Later she took my hand. I even recall her words. She said the bell was nice and thanked me for helping."

"Mama said you had the gift of comfort," Addie added, and Eli thought of his father's mention of an "angel" girl who prayed at his mother's burial. "We liked the bell," Addie went on. "It was sad, but we liked hearing the bell, like a song for my papa." She smiled then, and Eli looked away from her sweetness.

He could not stand all this sentimental talk. "You've plenty of money, I'd bet, to get folks to hop whenever you got a need." He began to move again, but the girls walked beside him now.

"My papa used to pay people to look after things, to shine the floors and all, but they all went away 'cept Sophie." Her voice broke. "Sophie must be awful sick, not to come back to me. Do you think Sophie's got dead too?"

Eli glanced down at the child. For a second he did not see Addie and her golden curls. He saw Molly's red braids, Molly alone and miserable, and he rubbed his eyes. Don't go soft, he told himself.

She's not Molly. If you get soft, you'll break. "No matter what happened to Sophie, you're an orphan now. There's lots of orphans," he said and his words were as hard as the shield he longed for. "The Howards see to orphans."

Addie shook her head. "I don't want to go to an orphans' asylum. I want to stay at my house and sleep in my bed. My aunt Elizabeth will come."

"Well then, Miss High and Mighty, it's clear you'll have to hire help. Don't know how you'll find a nursemaid in this city now, though." Eli stopped and looked at the Graveyard Girl. "Not unless Miss Grace knows someone."

But the Graveyard Girl had no chance to speak. "No," Addie blurted out. "The money's gone. Everything's gone 'cept the treasure. Mama said not to touch the treasure."

"Your mother sent you to me," said the Graveyard Girl. "She sent you for a reason. Don't worry. I think I know the perfect person to care for you."

Fine, thought Eli. You help her. Just leave me out of it, but he could feel both girls looking at him.

They walked in silence for a few steps, but then the Graveyard Girl spoke. "Eli will stay with you. He needs a roof over his head."

"Oh, no-o-o!" Eli stepped away from them. "I ain't fixing to take on no position as a nursemaid. No sirree. It's west I'm heading, getting away from the river and the fever, I am. Come first light tomorrow, Memphis won't be seeing nothing of Eli Mahoney save his back."

For a moment the Graveyard Girl said nothing. Her gray eyes seemed to see down inside him. Her voice, when she did speak, was soft. "You'll do what you must do, of course. Each of us does what his own heart directs." Then she cocked her eyebrow, and all seriousness was gone. "I just know for sure you won't turn your back on two ladies in distress." She smiled. "I just swear you're a regular gentleman."

Eli wanted to run away from this girl who was one minute an angel, the next a tease. He wanted to shout that he owed her nothing, that she knew nothing about him, had no hold over him, but it was not true. He was fettered somehow by the girl and by Elmwood Cemetery.

He could smell the oleander bush that grew near the sidewalk. He could see the sunset folding its pink around the tombstones in the eastern section. He could feel himself being held, and he was too tired to fight. "I'll stay tonight," he said, "just tonight."

"Good." The Graveyard Girl did not seem surprised. She bent down to Addie. "You've nothing to fear," she told the little girl.

Addie leaned close to the Graveyard Girl to half whisper. "Does Eli like me now?"

"Yes," said Grace, and Eli wanted to run.

"That's nice. I like Eli too, but . . ." Addie paused and her voice took on a worried tone. "My mama's going to think he's frightfully dirty."

Eli was glad for a reason to be angry. He looked down at himself. "You bet your sweet life I'm dirty, not that your mama's likely to notice." He flashed her a sarcastic smile. "Guess you wouldn't know, but a body gets dirty doing a real day's work." A thought came to him then, bringing a genuine smile. "I'll just soak myself clean tonight in your fancy bathtub. So let's get going."

"Not until Addie's had something to eat," said Grace, "unless, of course, you want to cook for her yourself."

"Not likely." Eli stomped ahead of them to the back of the cottage and settled himself on the stoop. He could hear the girls inside, Grace fussing over Addie, offering to butter more bread and pour the milk.

Spoiling the little brat even more, thought Eli. Well, she wouldn't get the royal treatment from me, not that I'll be hanging around that long. Still, while I'm here I'll not be making her into a blooming little princess. Good for the kid. Nobody had spoiled Molly. Sure, he had bought her peppermints when his fish brought a few extra pennies. He'd call to her from the road. "Hey, Molly, Molly Mahoney! I'd give a peppermint if I had me someone to tote my fishing pole."

Suddenly Eli jumped up from the stoop. He clenched his fists and fought the great moan that threatened to well up from inside him. "Hurry it up," he yelled to the girls inside. "I've no desire to be traipsing around in the dark."

When finally the Graveyard Girl had hugged Addie good-bye and they were moving, Eli did not slow his usual pace. At first Addie trotted to stay up with him, but before they were out of the Elmwood gate, she had slowed. "Wait for me. You walk too fast," she demanded. She stopped and folded her arms across her chest.

"I'm setting the stride," he muttered, but he slowed his steps.

Addie skipped to his side. At the curb, she reached out and wrapped her small hand around two of his fingers. It was the way Molly had always held his hand. The wild grief grew up inside Eli again. He fought to push it down, and he jerked his hand away from Addie. "No need to hold my hand just to cross a street now," he told her, and his voice was rough. "There's not a soul stirring. Not likely to be, either, except maybe some poor wore-out doctor or nurse. Memphis is dead, as dead as me."

"Don't be silly. You're not dead at all." She reached out and touched his leg. "See, I can touch you. That's how I know you're not dead. I can see Mama when she comes into my room, but I can't touch her. I wish I could touch my Mama just one more time."

"Look," said Eli. "I know how you feel. My own mother's buried back there at Elmwood, and it's a sure thing I'm wishing I could touch her myself, but there will be no talk about your mother coming into your room. Not to me." He bent and put his hands on her shoulders. "Your mother is dead and buried. Dead people don't go sashaying around into rooms to visit. Once they're dead, they stay dead. You get this straight. Any more talk about visits from your dead mother and I'll run off and leave you all alone in the night. Understand?"

Addie stared him full in the face. For a second Eli thought she would defy him, but then she nodded her blond head solemnly. "Very well. I won't mention Mama's visits to you any more, but I'll have to talk to her about you because she will ask who the strange boy is when she comes into my room tonight."

Eli groaned and began to walk again. "It's daft you are, just plain daft."

"Daft?" Addie did a little skip. "I don't know

that word. Is it a compliment? Mama always says a lady must thank a gentleman for a compliment."

"Humph," was Eli's only response.

The house, when they reached it, was even grander than Eli remembered. Thinking back to the day when he had sold fish at the back door, he marveled how drastically life had changed. Both the master and the mistress of this great house were dead now, the servants gone. Eli's mother and little sister were dead too. That day, the other time he had come to this house, Eli had fished with his father.

When they were on the porch, Addie's voice broke into his thoughts. "It makes me feel sad," said the little girl. "Coming home with no mama or papa here."

Eli nodded. Into his mind flashed the picture of his home, dark and vacant now, with no one left to hear the sounds of the lonely river. "It's bad everywhere." The words came out softer, sadder than he had intended, and he determined to stiffen.

He took her shoulder and turned her toward the street. No one moved. There came to their ears the great boom of a cannon, fired by city officials several times each night in an effort to purify the air from the fever's poison. Fires up and down the street marked where the bed things of the dead were being burned.

A woman's scream came from somewhere

down the block. "No! Oh, God, no! My baby, my baby!"

"Another little coffin needed, I reckon," said Eli, and again he was glad there was no feeling left inside him. "See what I mean, girlie? Whole city is dying. You and me, we're alive for right now. Might not be before long, but it don't matter, anyhow."

They were at the door, but Addie stepped in front of it. "Don't you be talking like that in this house," she demanded. "My mama won't like you at all if you're going to be talking like that." Then she smiled. "Besides, you matter to me, Eli. You matter a big bunch to me."

Five

ELI PUSHED THE GREAT DOOR, AND IT OPENED INTO
a wide hall. It was a silent house, a house filled
with shadows. This time he did not object as
Addie slipped her hand into his. When his eyes
had adjusted to the dimness, he sucked in his
breath with surprise. He had been at the back
doors of Memphis's elegant homes but had never
glimpsed the splendor inside.

He stood staring at the grand chandelier, the
thick rugs, the luxurious furniture, delicate vases,
and lamps. "Like a blooming cathedral," Eli whispered. "My da took me in St. Peter's once. Not
much grander than this place."

After Addie showed him how to start the
gaslights, he wandered for a time, peering into
room after room. She followed him into one of
the smaller rooms. At the center stood a rich
walnut piece of furniture with ivory keys.

Eli, who had inherited his father's love of music, felt drawn toward the instrument. He touched a key. "Mama's melodeon," said Addie. "This is her music room. She still comes here sometimes at night after she leaves my room, and she plays her favorite songs."

He slammed the cover down over the keys. "It's off to bed with you. No argument neither. I've had all I can stand of your daffy talk."

She smiled. "I never fuss about bedtime. It's my favorite part, because Mama comes right after I go to sleep."

"Exactly! You dream. Sure you've had dreams before."

"I know about dreams, silly." She turned up her nose in what Eli thought was a sassy look. "I'm six years old. Dreams are stories in your head while you're sleeping, but dreams aren't real."

"That's right, and you dream about your mother coming into your room."

Addie shrugged her little shoulders. "Grace told me you can't understand about Mama. You ought to understand more than I do because you're pretty big, but Grace says you'll learn."

"All I'm wanting to learn is what California looks like, maybe how gold feels in my own hand, but I've no wish to argue with a daft little girl. To bed with you."

"Maybe you'll see Mama too." Addie smiled

softly. "She's very pretty, and she has on a long white dress. It's her wedding dress, and Sophie put it on her before they took her away in the box."

Eli shook his head. No use to protest, he thought. Still, after Addie was in her bed, and he was in the fine bathroom, he found himself listening for any unusual sound. He had never before seen water come from a pipe, and it fascinated him. He wanted to fill the tub, but the way the water's noise blocked out other sounds made him uneasy.

"Thieves," she said aloud. "It's thieves I'm worried about; fancy place like this, it's a miracle looters haven't come in and carried away every last thing." He had seen the yellow cards that signaled fever in the house. While the water ran, he went back to find them lying on a table and posted one on each door. "There," he said. "Thieves ain't likely to come into a house where they think folks has the jack." But back in the bathroom he could not relax, despite the way the cool water washed away the dirt and soothed his muscles.

The room across from Addie's was a guest room with a big four-poster all made up with clean linen, and it was there that Eli bedded down. Under different circumstances, he would have enjoyed the luxury, would have felt important sleeping in such an elegant bed instead of on his narrow cot. Now, however, there was no feeling left in him except exhaustion.

He lay in the great bed waiting for sleep and watching the moon play on the velvet curtains. His eyes were just about closed when the sound came, causing him to sit upright in bed. What was it? What had jerked him back from the edge of sleep? He got up and crept to the door. There it was again, and he knew it came from Addie's room. It was a voice, someone talking. No! Two people were talking. A chill went up Eli's spine.

Tiptoeing, he opened his door and moved across the hall to Addie's. Pressing his ear against the wood, he held his breath and listened. The voices were plainer now, but still he could not make out words. With a shaking hand, he turned the knob and inched open the door.

"I won't, Mama. I won't forget." It was Addie's voice.

Moonlight filled the room, and Eli saw the little girl sitting up in the big canopy bed with a pink spread. Go on in, he told himself, but his feet did not move. "Addie," he was still standing in the doorway. "Who are you talking to, girl?"

The little girl said nothing. Instead she sat staring out across the room. He crossed to her, put out his hand, and shook her shoulder. "What's wrong with you? Can't you hear? Answer me."

He was unprepared for her response. Suddenly

she jumped from the bed and ran to the window. "Mama," she screamed. "Mama, where did you go? Oh, come back to me, Mama. Oh please, please come back to me."

The words gripped Eli's heart. They were the very words he wanted to scream into the night. "Mama, come back. Please come back to me." He crossed the room to Addie, thinking perhaps he would comfort her, put an arm around her as he used to put his arms around Molly. "There, there," he said and reached for her.

She whirled toward him, but she did not turn for comfort. "You hateful, hateful boy." She pounded against his chest with her fists. "Why'd you have to come in and chase Mama away? She'd have stayed. She would have stayed with me except you came in! I hate you. I hate you."

Eli grabbed the little girl's wrists. "Stop, you little fool. You'll get a whopping across my knee yet."

Addie stopped fighting and started to cry. "It's true," she sobbed. "My mama would have stayed 'cept for you. Now she's gone." She wiped her eyes and folded her arms across her chest. "Well, I just will not tell you what she said about the treasure. I just most certainly will not."

Eli's knees felt weak. He looked around the room. There had been two voices. Only one of them had been Addie's. Could it be true? Could her mother have been in the room? He squinted his eyes, staring hard into the dark corner.

She was watching him, waiting, he realized, to argue about something. "Huh?" he asked. "What is it you're threatening to do?"

"I won't tell you what Mama said about the treasure she hid away. Mama said not to touch the treasure unless I had to have money. She said if I had to have it to ask the Graveyard Girl to help me dig under the rosebush." Addie turned up her chin defiantly.

Despite his uneasiness, a grin came to Eli's lips. "So you'll get even with me all right. You won't tell me where the treasure is that's buried under the rosebush. You're sure enough going to get even with me, I reckon."

Addie realized her mistake and clapped her small palm across her mouth. She turned away from Eli, pushed open the window, and leaned out, looking into the night.

With a great sigh of exasperation, he grabbed up her small body. "I'm fixing to pack you off to bed, and you best stay there if you know what's good for you." He stomped to the bed, where he dropped her hard onto the pink spread. "It's too weary I am to stand in the night listening to your windjammer talk about dead mothers coming to tell you about treasures."

Eli walked to the door without looking back

at Addie, but before going out he leaned against the door facing to collect himself. He determined to ignore the sounds from the bed.

Addie was crying softly. "Mama," he heard her say. "Please come back. He's gone now. That boy is gone."

He went out the door and slammed it behind him, but he disliked how still he stood in the hallway, how he strained to hear, holding his breath. It's all right, he told himself when no sound came to him except the sobs of the child. I've heard enough crying, he thought, and went back to his room, fell across the bed, and reached for sleep.

And sleep did come to his exhausted body, but just as drowsiness was about to wrap him in sweet forgetfulness, he heard a voice, a soft voice singing, "Light and rosy be thy slumber, Rock'd up-on thy mother's breast, She can lull thee with her numbers, To the cradled heav'n of rest."

He could hear the words faintly and the keys of the melodeon. He rolled over. The singing was not in his room. It came through the open door from a room downstairs. Get up, he told himself, but his weary legs did not respond to the order. The voice was so gentle, the music so sweet. His eyes were too heavy, and they closed.

A dream came to him, a dream of his mother. She sat in the old rocking chair near the window.

Molly was on her lap. Eli stood outside the window, but the words of the lullaby drifted clearly to him.

He had never heard his mother sing the song before, and he wanted to ask her where she had learned it. He opened the door and called to her. "Ma, what's that song? It's new, ain't it?"

The woman in the dream turned to him, and he was surprised to see that it was not, after all, his mother. It was Addie's mother, the face from the portrait downstairs.

"Get away, you awful boy. Get away." It was Addie, not Molly, on the woman's lap.

In the dream, he began to cry. "Don't cry," he thought, hating himself for letting Addie and her mother see his weakness. "Tears won't do you one little whit of good." Still he cried, great loud sobs.

He woke then. The house was quiet and dark. A great heaviness filled his chest. He remembered the dream, remembered the feeling of letting go. He could cry now, he knew. There was no one to see him. His eyes, though, remained dry. He lay in the dark, longing for his mother, and wishing even for the comfort of tears.

Six

ELI SLEPT FITFULLY, BUT STILL HE WOKE BEFORE dawn. It was time for him to be up and on his way out of Memphis. Let someone else deal with the girl and the voices that came in the night. Eli was sick of thinking of it. Today he would start his trip west. He wasn't exactly sure how he'd go about it, but he had to leave the city behind.

He stretched, yawned, and looked around the room. Heavy curtains hung at the windows. A fine pewter pitcher sat in a bowl on the washstand. "Bring hot water." Eli snapped his fingers at an imaginary servant. "Be quick with you." He wondered how it would feel to be wealthy, to live in a big house, and be waited on by others.

Addie had always enjoyed the life of the rich. Surely there was money still in her father's business accounts. The kid would be fine when her aunt came to get everything straightened out. She would just have to survive in an orphans' asylum until the woman arrived.

He looked about the room at the silver candle-sticks and the shiny bedside tray. If the house stood empty, looters would take everything. Even the soft, thick rugs would likely be stripped off the floors.

So what? The Graveyard Girl would try to make him stay, and she was strangely hard to refuse. Maybe he would not announce his departure. Maybe he would deliver Addie to Elmwood, wait until Grace was busy, and then disappear.

Yes, he would be on his way today. Addie Carlile and her house were not his problem. Let her dig up the treasure if there really was one under the rosebush.

He got up and walked to the rear window to look out over the back garden. Light was beginning to show in the east. Eli could see that there were beds of yellow, red, and white flowers, but only one rosebush, full of pink blossoms.

He studied the bush. What if there really was a treasure buried there? Hadn't he heard someone talking to Addie in the night? Still, even if the treasure existed, it wouldn't mean Addie had been told about it by a dead woman. Maybe Addie's mother had buried valuables before she died. Maybe Addie had even helped her, or maybe the whole thing was some sort of dream. It might be interesting to see.

The house was quiet. Addie would sleep for hours yet. He could slip out into the garden without the little girl ever knowing. For a time he resisted, moving about the room touching the finery, going into the bathroom to marvel once more at the running water, but always coming back to the window for another look at the rosebush.

Then he made up his mind. Very quietly he went out his door and to the back stairway. "Let's have a dig for your treasure, Mrs. Ghost Lady," he whispered, and the creak of the stairs under his step made a shiver move up his back.

Outside, Eli paused for a minute to survey the garden more closely. It was still beautiful, but it had obviously been neglected. Weeds grew among the flowers, and the grass along the walks was out of control. The gardener must have been one of the first to go, he thought. Only the rosebush seemed unaffected. Full of pink flowers, it held its blooms, gentle but proud, just as it always had, unaware of the misery around it.

Ma would have loved a garden like this, Eli thought, even just one rosebush. She would have touched the first buds and waited happily for them to turn into flowers. He shook his head. He did not want to start thinking of his mother, not if he was going to dig up some other mother's treasure. There was no doubt what his mother would think of such actions.

Still, he moved toward the roses. Before bending down to examine the dirt beneath the bush, he looked over his shoulder toward the house. Watching for the girl or for her mother? he asked himself. Again the shiver went up his spine.

A gardener's shed stood back beside the fence, and there Eli found a shovel. "Surprised some looter hasn't latched on to this. Burying's in big demand these days," he said, and the sound of his own voice made him feel less uneasy.

With one eye on the house, he began to dig, pushing hard against the shovel. "Fancy lady like her not likely to have lasted digging too long," he muttered, and he was right. A thumping sound came when his blade touched something more than dirt. Gently he maneuvered the shovel until he could see it, a small wooden box.

Eli sucked in his breath. His knees shook, and he knelt down for a better look. The box was a heavy dark wood with intricate carvings, and he could imagine that it must have sat on the lady's dressing table.

He put out his hand to lift the box, but a voice in his head stopped him. "It ain't yours." His mother's words with their accusing tone were as plain to him as his own words had been. "You've no business messing with what ain't yours," she added.

"I'm just looking, Ma. Just looking," he whispered. Then he threw up his hands in exasperation. "I've turned as daft as Addie, setting here carrying on a conversation with my dead mother." He shook his head and reached for the box.

Quickly, before anything could stop him, he pulled at the lid. Jewelry! Sparkling jewelry. In the box was a golden bracelet, a brooch with shiny stones, two glowing rings, and a string of pearls.

Eli touched the gleaming valuables, held them up to catch the first light of morning. Addie's mother had worn these, likely even her grandmother had, worn them to grand balls and elegant parties.

Afraid of thieves, she must have come out here in the night to dig for a safe spot. Had she been sick already then? Had she known she was dying and hidden these things away for her daughter? Had Addie been with her, or had her mother told her later? Had she died before she had a chance to tell the child? Had she really come back to guide her child to the treasure?

A sudden breeze came to the garden, lifting the damp hair from Eli's forehead and making the pink flowers sway on the rosebush. She's here, he thought, but he scolded himself for such a foolish idea.

He liked the brooch best. Trembling, he ran his fingers across the bright stones in their gold background. There were green ones and red ones and several that were clear and shiny. "Them's diamonds. I'll just bet them is diamonds," he whispered. His father had talked often of a diamond ring worn by his grandmother in better days back in Ireland's County Fermanagh, back when the Mahoney name had been a proud one.

Maybe he could just stick it in his pocket. Wouldn't there be plenty left? Likely the little girl would just dig the things up when her aunt came and this trouble was all over. Likely the aunt had money of her own, and wasn't there bound to be something left of Addie's father's business? Even if the treasure had to be sold, there would be enough.

Why shouldn't he just slip the brooch in his pocket? He would leave the rest, cover it back over and let it be. But the brooch. Why shouldn't he take it?

"You know why, son." His mother's answer came at once to his head. "You want to think about proud names, study on this. The Mahoneys was never thieves, not any of my people either." He could imagine his mother standing in front of him, watching.

He felt torn, wanting to please his mother, but knowing how much the brooch could mean to him. Of course he couldn't sell it in Memphis.

Jewelers and all other businesses were closed. He might be able to trade it for something, but it would be best to keep the piece in his pocket until he was out of the city. Then he would take it to a proper shopkeeper and get real money. He wouldn't be quick either. He'd check around until he found the best price. Eli Mahoney's no fool, he thought.

He picked up the brooch and moved it toward his pants pocket. "You're no thief, neither." It was his mother's voice again, and the words seemed so real that they made him jump.

"I've got to, Ma," he said. "I know you'd hate it powerful, but I got to. This yellow jack has changed things. It's got me stumped, and I just got to borrow this brooch. I'll pay back every last penny. I will, Ma."

His heart was pounding, but his hand would work. The brooch was almost in the pocket when another voice came, a living voice from the house.

"Eli, Eli, where are you?" It was Addie, awake and running from room to room, calling his name.

He gritted his teeth. He had to get the box covered over again, quick. Stuff the brooch in your pocket and get the box back now, he told himself.

"There is no excuse for doing wrong, boy. You're stronger than the fever."

"Oh, no, Ma. I'm not. You don't know," he said, but he threw the brooch back into the box, replaced it beneath the roses, took the shovel, and tossed dirt once more into the hole.

He had just returned the shovel and stood sweating, when Addie came bounding out the back door. She had on her nightgown, and her doll was in her arms.

"There you are." She sounded relieved, and she moved toward him as if she might hug him. "I'm so glad. I called and called, but no one came." She shuddered. "I thought you had gone away and left me all by myself."

"No." He jammed his hands into his pockets and looked once more toward the rosebush. "I'm still here."

"I'm awful glad." She moved toward him.

He stepped back. "Yeah. Well, you weren't so crazy about me last night. Remember?"

"I'm sorry." She hung her head. "I guess I was real ugly to you." She paused, searching for words. "I just got all fired up because Mama went away when you came in. Are you mad at me?"

"Look." He shoved past her. "Some little feisty girl ain't about to trouble me over much. I don't care about what you imagine your dead mother says to you in the night, neither. I'm leaving here. I'm going out West."

He expected her to cry, to grab on to his hand, and he whirled to look back at her.

She was smiling. "You won't leave me." Her words were very soft.

"What?" he shouted.

"I said you won't leave me. You will live right here with me and be my brother."

His blood boiled. For a minute he considered hitting her, but of course he wouldn't. She was small, as small as Molly. Still, he could not have her trying to hold on to him, trying to make him care about her. "No," he said. "I will not live here. I had me a little sister, but she is buried now in Elmwood Cemetery. I've no wish to get mixed up with a daft little thing like you."

"I think you'll stay," she said. "My mama just whispered in my ear, and she told me you will stay."

Seven

"LOOKS LIKE RAIN," ELI SAID WHEN THEY WERE ON their way to Elmwood Cemetery. "We'd better hurry." While Addie dressed, he had waited on the back porch, watching the clouds and laying his plan. He would take the little girl to Grace. Then, without telling either of the girls that he was going, he would sneak away, go back to Carlile House, dig up the treasure, borrow the brooch, and head west.

"Does the Graveyard Girl ring the bell even in the rain?" Addie asked, but she did not press him when his only answer was a shrug of his shoulders.

It was no longer so early. The city should have been stirring by now, early shoppers going to market, wagons full of goods moving down toward the river docks. But the streets were quiet, almost as deserted as the night before.

Even Addie seemed to be affected by the silence, and by the darkness of the sky. Only the sound of her hard breathing accompanied the noise of their feet on the board streets. The quiet was interrupted, though, when they reached Elmwood.

Even before they were inside the white picket fence, the racket of Memphis's busiest place came to their ears. Shovels struck against hard earth and stones as digging crews prepared graves, and Grace was already ringing the bell for the people who had been delivered the day before, after closing time.

There was the clatter of wheels, too, as McLemore headed the big wagon toward them. Eli raised his hand in greeting, and the man reined in the great horses.

"Eli, ain't it?" He tipped his hat toward Addie. "A fine lady with you. Who is this little miss?"

"Addie. Addie Carlile's her name." He motioned back toward the direction from which they had come. "Her place's over there, but her folks was took by the jack."

"Sorry, Miss." McLemore's voice was gentle. "Knowed your papa I did. Worked a bit for him around his warehouse."

Addie smiled. "Papa's warehouse. You know my papa's warehouse?" She pointed off in the direction of the river. "I used to go there, and we would have picnics by the water. I loved Papa's warehouse, all big and filled with cotton. It was fun to play hide-and-seek there."

McLemore leaned toward the little girl, giving her his full attention, but Eli was impatient. He jerked her hand. "Rattles on, she does. Where's your helper?"

"Fever's struck him." He shook his head. "Folks dropping worse than in the war. Not going to be nobody left. Pray for that there frost, young-uns. We got to all pray for early frost. Got to get now, see can I find me another helper 'fore the storm hits." He took up the reins and called, "Get up," to urge the horses on.

Eli began to walk, but Addie stood still, start-ing after the wagon. "You coming?" he called, but still she did not stir. Her lips moved, but he could not hear and had to step back beside her. "What? For pete's sake speak up."

"Everybody's getting the fever." Her voice was shaky. She pointed toward the digging crew. "Everybody's getting buried. That man said so. He said there wouldn't be nobody left." Her body began to shake, and she put her hand across her eyes. "Eli, will you get dead? Will you, Eli?"

His heart softened, and he brushed his hand lightly over her hair. "No, he said, "I've had the jack, same as you, in seventy-three."

A smile lit her face, and the bounce came back at once to her body. Eli opened his mouth to add that his health would make no difference in her life, that he was leaving Memphis anyway, but she skipped forward and took his hand. She looked up at him with such happiness, her eyes big and blue like Molly's.

Eli started to push her away, but she put her arm up around his waist and settled for a minute against him. He bit his lip. Be careful, he told himself, you can't start taking to the little scamp. You're better off not giving a hoot about nobody. "Can't you understand?" he said. "I ain't aiming to hang around here."

"Oh, don't go off, Eli. Please don't go off and leave me."

The pain on her face made him look away. He would definitely have to get out of Elmwood without her knowing. "You hungry?" he asked. "I'll bet Miss Grace has got us some breakfast cooked."

The bell had stopped ringing, and the Graveyard Girl stood waiting for them by the time they reached the cottage step. "I've saved grits on the stove for you," she said when Addie ran to her. "Come on in and eat."

Eli stomped behind the girls. Grace moved to the big book spread across the table and began to write. Hunger rolled inside Eli's stomach. Two bowls sat beside the kettle of grits. Addie was filling one before Eli was completely through the door.

"Here." She held the dish out to him. "Here, you take this one. I'll get me another one."

"No," said Eli. He started to add that he would rather get his own, but the disappointment on her face made him stop. He smiled at her. "Well, I'll take it if you want. That's right nice of you."

They were both at the table eating when Addie spoke to the Graveyard Girl. "Mama came to me again last night," she said.

Eli did not stop eating, but he made a snorting sound, and Addie turned to him. "You're being mean again. Don't be mean, please," she pleaded. "Didn't you hear her? Didn't you hear Mama talking to me just before you came in?"

The boy thought quickly as he swallowed. He had heard two voices, hadn't he? An answer came to him. "You were playacting," he announced. "You've got an imagination like my little sister. Molly used to do playacting for hours. She'd hold up her doll, Janie. 'Darlin', she'd say, 'it's time for you to go to bed now.' Then she'd talk for the doll, arguing and begging to stay up. Molly was good at pretend and at voices. She was. From outside the room, through a door and all, she could have fooled a sleepy-headed person, made him think two people talked." He nodded his head with satisfaction and began to eat his grits again.

"Eli," Grace asked, "why do you refuse to believe Addie's mother comes to her?" There was no anger, no accusation in her voice, and suddenly Eli felt as if he might cry.

He knew the answer well, and he wanted to tell it, to spill out the hurt inside. But he also wanted to gain control of himself before he did.

His hunger was gone, and he pushed back his bowl of grits and stood before he began to speak. "I know Addie's mother don't come to her because mine don't come to me." There was no anger in his voice, only conviction, sure and certain. "If anyone could return from the dead my mother would come to me. She would never have left me alone to watch Molly die. My little sister held my hand, she did. She held my hand, and she asked me to make her head quit hurting. Me beside her, my body aching with tiredness. Still, it wasn't tiredness made me shake. It was heartbreak, my heart broke all to pieces inside me. Could any soul come back after death, it would be my ma. She'd have stood beside me when I realized my da wasn't going to be any help at all. She'd have touched my hair like she done when I fretted over something. 'You're not alone, Eli,' she used to say. 'You're never alone.' My mother would come to me was it possible for anyone to come."

He stopped talking and looked at the girls. Addie had her head down on the table. Grace made no attempt to hide her tears. "Oh, Eli," she said softly. "Oh, Eli."

Slowly he turned, and with purposeful steps he marched from the cottage. The water that hit his face and began at once to soak his clothes surprised him. So lost had he been in his story that he had not noticed the rain had started. It fell from the sky as if a great curtain of gray had been unrolled.

Eli could hardly see, and for a minute he considered going back into the cottage. Instead he made his way toward the small chapel. Just as he reached the carved oak door, a voice came to him. "Eli," Grace called. "Eli, where are you?"

"Please come back, Eli," Addie too cried out into the rain, but Eli pushed on into the chapel, closed the door behind him, and leaned against it. After he caught his breath and wiped the water from his face, he moved to the other end of the room and onto a small platform, which held a large pulpit. He had thought to sit behind it, but was glad to discover that he could actually crawl inside the podium.

The temperature was dropping. Eli, wet and shivering, hugged his knees close. If Grace and Addie came looking for him, they would not guess where he hid. He had opened himself up, laid out his agony on the cottage table. He did not want to see them again. He would wait, he told himself, until the rain let up. Then he would go. He would go far away.

A noise disturbed his thoughts. Eli could hear the door opening, and he peeked out to see two men carrying wooden coffins between them. "We got to stack 'em," one declared. "Ain't going to be room otherwise."

Eli listened to the tromping of feet and the sound of wood on wood as the digging crew carried in box after box. "Could of left a few," one voice complained. "Rain wouldn't of been no matter to the dead, but no, that girl wouldn't have it."

"Stop your whining," snapped his companion. "It's clear you're new around here. We don't hold with no throwing off on the Graveyard Girl. You must be glad you're not in a box like these poor stiffs."

When finally the men stopped coming, Eli crawled out from his hiding place. Wooden coffins were stacked on the benches and lined the walls. He went to the window and saw a large wagon full of men rolling toward the gate. "They want to get away," he said aloud. "They want to get away and go back to the living." He wished he had asked for a ride.

Well, he would just wait. The dead didn't

bother him. Wasn't he one of them, really? He made his way back to the speaker stand and crawled inside once again. The sound of the rain on the roof lulled him. With his head bent over to his knees, he decided to close his eyes.

After he woke, his brain was fuzzy. For one terrifying moment, he thought he had been stuffed into a small coffin, but then he realized he could crawl out of his box. The cramps in his legs and neck told him that he had slept for quite a time.

He made his way again to the window. The rain still fell in great sheets, but Eli could see the cottage. A lamp stood near the cottage window, and he knew that the small front room was bright despite the gray afternoon. Addie walked by the glass, then the Graveyard Girl.

A longing struck Eli. They're alive in there, he thought, and I'm here with all the dead. "So? Ain't this what you like? Ain't you glad to be away from them?"

He tried to pull himself away from the window. Maybe he could count the coffins or even go back to sleep. Maybe he should just ignore the rain and start walking out of Memphis.

"Eli."

"Eli."

They were at the door of the cottage again, and their voices reached out to him through the wet grayness. If you go there, you'll be trapped, he warned himself, but he knew he would go.

He forced his way around the coffin and ran out into the rain, ran faster than he ever had, toward the lighted cottage. The Graveyard Girl must have heard him coming, because she held open the door, and Addie clapped and jumped with delight as he entered.

Eight

ALL AFTERNOON THE RAIN BEAT AGAINST THE BROWN
cottage. Eli, his stomach full of beans and corn
bread, sat quietly in the corner watching as Grace
gave Addie a sewing lesson.

The blue satin covered the table. Addie put
down her needle and the scrap piece of material
she had practiced stitching. "Will there be dancing
at the party?" she asked.

"Oh, yes," said Grace, "the Virginia reel."

"Can I go to the party?" Addie left her chair
and went over to lean against Grace. "Will you
teach me to dance the Ginia reel?"

"I promise," said the Graveyard Girl. "After
the frost comes, we'll just dance and dance."

"Eli too," said the little girl. "I want Eli to
dance too."

He could feel Grace's gray eyes boring into
him, and for a moment he did not meet her gaze.

Neither of the girls had asked him where he had gone when he ran out into the rain. All afternoon neither of them had talked about dead mothers or pressed him about his plans. Now the unasked questions seemed to fill the room.

Eli knew the answer. He knew he would stay in Memphis. He raised his head, and he smiled at the Graveyard Girl.

"Yes," Grace told Addie. "Eli too. On the morning of the first frost, we'll all dance together. We . . ."

Her words were interrupted by a call from the other room. "Gracie, Gracie girl, come please."

She stood and went at once toward her father's room. "He's stronger," she said. "Sat up for a time earlier and ate a good bowl of beans." Eli saw happiness spread across her face.

"It's cooler," Addie said to Eli. "Maybe the frost will come tonight."

He shook his head. " 'Fraid not. The rain's made it cool off for today. That's likely all. Probably be at least another month before the first hard frost."

Addie touched the satin. "Well, Grace can finish her dress by then. She can wear her blue dress when we dance."

Eli said nothing. There too much hurt inside him to imagine dancing, but down among the anguish was a tiny forecast of hope. Addie yawned and moved across the room to curl into the only comfortable chair, a big cushioned rocker.

"While Grace's with her papa, I'll just rest my eyes," she said. "Then when she's ready, I'll help some more with the sewing." She yawned again and put her head down on the soft arm. "We got to have it ready for the dancing."

Addie was asleep when Grace came back into the room. Eli went over to open the door. "Rain's almost stopped," he said. "Guess I ought to get Addie to her bed."

"Wait till it's really stopped. I could make us a cup of tea." She filled the teakettle, and Eli closed the door. "There's still a little chill in the air. We could have an early frost. We really could. I'll ask Papa about the earliest one he can recall."

They were quiet until the kettle began to whistle. "You know, Eli, you're lucky to have memories of your mother."

Eli pushed back the bench from where he had settled at the table. "I don't want to set into talking about my ma."

"It was not my intention"—she wrinkled her nose at him and handed him a cup—"not my intention at all to make you talk about anything. I was going to tell you about my mother."

"Sorry," muttered Eli, and he slid back down on the bench. "I'd be pleased to hear."

"She died the day I was born, the moment after, actually." Grace sat down across from him, her hands wrapped around her cup. "They say Mama knew she couldn't last. She'd come down with consumption, grew weaker and weaker, but she held to life so her babe could live. When she heard me cry, she said, 'A girl, by the grace of God, I've given life to a little girl.' Then she died."

"That's real sorrowful." Eli stared at his cup.

"Yes, but strangely, as a child I didn't see it quite that way. Maybe it was because I'd never known a mother. Anyway, instead of sad, I felt special, sanctified somehow by her death. My father named me Grace because of what she said, and he told me I was marked by God." She laughed slightly. "This probably sounds peculiar to you, but I grew up beside my mother's grave. I'd take my dinner there to eat or my lessons to do. Sometimes I'd hear a sort of whisper in the trees of Elmwood, like God's voice telling me I had a mission in life."

Eli remembered a picture in a book Father Fitzhugh had shown him, Saint Joan, a girl of seventeen, called by God to free France. He wanted to tell Grace about Saint Joan, to say that Grace was like her, but he could not find the words. "You've fought the fever," he said. "In all of Memphis no bell save yours has rung for the dead."

She smiled at him. "Thank you." She stood and moved over to the window. "Eli," she almost whispered, "I'm going to tell you something I've never said to another soul. I've dreams of being a doctor."

"You mean a nurse?"

She whirled back to him. "No, oh, no, I mean a doctor. Sister Agnes says I'm bright. She says I'm bright enough to do anything. There's a woman named Elizabeth Blackwell, she's a doctor and her sister too. Sister Agnes told me about their clinic in New York City, a place for poor women and children. Some men folks didn't want Elizabeth Blackwell to be a doctor, but she became one anyway." Her voice dropped even lower. "I might do that too. I might become a doctor."

"You could," he said, "I vow you could."

"When the fever's gone, when it's all over, I'm going to talk to Sister Agnes about it."

The wind came up just then, blowing through the trees of Elmwood Cemetery. Eli listened, and thought that he too might be hearing the voice of God.

"Eli." Addie's voice pulled him back.

"I'm here." Going to her, he knelt beside the chair. "Get on," he told her. "I'm fixing to give you a piggyback ride to your bed."

Grace draped a blanket around them. "In case the rain starts again," she said.

Clouds made the evening sky much darker than usual. When a distant dog howled mournfully, Eli felt his own misery pushing against his insides. It's better to feel nothing, he told himself, but Addie snuggled warmly against his back, defying his thoughts.

When she was in bed, Addie called to him. "I'll be quiet tonight," she said. "Don't worry, no talking will wake you up."

"Good," he said. She's giving up her foolishness, he thought as he went down the stairs. In one room books lined the walls. Eli took one from a shelf, opened it, and looked at the words. He could read some, but his schooling had been limited, a fact that troubled his da.

On a July evening, only two months ago, Eli and his da had fished late, after Thomas had come from the dock, just before dark. Eli remembered how his father had sung about the shamrock and about St. Patrick.

A twilight breeze had come from the water, and Eli took off his shirt, leaned back in the skiff, and closed his eyes. The catch was good, the air was cool, and his father was singing. What more could he ask for? "I'll get a good price tonight, I'll wager," he had told his father when the song was done.

"Aye." Thomas had laid his hand on his son's shoulder. "But it's more than peddlin' fish I want for you, lad. You've a good wit about you. It's a fine businessman or maybe a mayor I'd see you be. School's what's needed. School. I'll be lookin' into more schooling for ye, lad. Come fall, I'll be findin' a way. I will.''

Eli shoved the book back onto the shelf. "All you found was a way to run out on me, wasn't it, Da." Anger threatened to explode inside him. He put out the lights and tromped up to bed. Sleep, maybe he could forget while he slept.

Addie kept her word, and nothing disturbed Eli in the night. When he woke, he remembered the treasure in the back garden. He did go to the window to look down at the rosebush, but he did not consider sneaking down to take the brooch. The previous morning seemed like a long time ago, and his cheeks burned with shame that he had ever thought of stealing from the little girl.

She was up and ready to go to the cemetery when he went into her room. "I want to help Grace sew," she announced.

"Most likely won't be time for sewing," Eli told her. "Lots of work got to go on at Elmwood today, making up for yesterday."

But Addie's spirits were not easily dampened. "This could be the last day of the fever," she announced. "It could be."

"No." Eli shook his head. "This won't be the last day, but that last day will come. It will." He was amazed because he believed his own words. The fever would pass, and someday so would the agony it had caused.

"We slept late," Eli told her as they started their walk. "See, the sun's high already."

"I didn't wake you up in the night either," she said.

He looked at her closely. "So there wasn't no one visiting you last night?"

She twisted her face slightly. "Well, well, I've decided not to talk to you about Mama anymore." She reached for his hand. "I don't want to make you feel sad, Eli."

He tried to smile a little and turned his attention to avoiding puddles left from yesterday's rain.

The burial crew was hard at work when they reached Elmwood, and the Graveyard Girl sat at her table with the big book. "I've had no time for cooking," she told Eli and Addie, "but we've lots of corn bread left and there's milk."

Eli noticed Grace's eyes were not as bright as usual. "Did you rest good last night?" he asked.

She brushed her hand across her face. "Do I look tired?" She did not wait for an answer. "It's just that we started work right after dawn. We've already buried fifty people this morning." She leaned her head on the table.

"I'll help you," Eli said. "Let me record the names. You rest."

She raised her head. "Eat first." She rose and went to the rocker. "I've folded away my cot, but maybe I'll just take my ease for a time."

Eli crumbled the bread into a glass of milk for Addie. "We made many a meal of cornpone and sweet milk at my house." The image of his ma, da, and Molly around the table with him flashed into his mind, and he wondered if he could swallow his food.

"There was a kitten out by the chapel this morning, Addie," Grace said, "a dear little yellow thing. I gave it some milk to drink. Thought you might like to play with it."

"When we're done here, I'll help you find it," said Eli. "Maybe Grace could get a little nap. Then I'll come back in and write the names."

Grace was asleep before they finished their milk, and they tiptoed out.

"She's not sick? Grace isn't sick, is she?" Addie pulled at his sleeve when they were outside.

Eli too had been afraid that her cheeks were redder than usual, but he shook his head. "Just tired. We'll help her every way we can today."

The kitten was on the walk, and Addie ran gleefully to swoop it up. Eli left her then and went to the graves of Molly and his mother.

"At least you're here together," he said after he had dropped to the strip between the mounds. He looked at the smaller grave. Poor little Molly, she'd have been afraid among strangers. "Don't be afraid, Puddin'." His words were familiar. He searched his mind and found the night not long before the fever had come to his mother.

"I'm afraid." Molly had sat up on her cot in the corner of the room. Eli had been working late by lamplight on his fishing net. "I had a bad dream."

"Dreams can't hurt you. Don't be afraid, Puddin'."

"Will you sing to me? I won't be afraid if you sing to me."

"Lay back down, then." He crossed to her cot and settled himself at the foot. He did not mind singing.

Remembering, he closed his eyes and began to sing again. This time it was to comfort himself.

> *Lavender's blue, dilly, dilly,*
> *Lavender's green.*
> *When I am king, dilly, dilly,*
> *You shall be queen.*
> *Call up your men, dilly, dilly,*
> *Set them to work,*
> *Some to the plough, dilly, dilly.*
> *Some to the cart.*

For a time he was lost in the song and the memories. He was totally unaware of Addie, who had wandered with her kitten to a bench beneath a tree a few feet from Molly's grave. But something made Eli look up to see the Graveyard Girl walking toward him. The girl moved quietly, almost as if her breath were held, her eyes looked beyond Eli, and she put her finger to her lips as a signal of silence.

A strange feeling came over Eli, and he felt compelled to go on singing. "Some to make hay, dilly, dilly, Some to cut corn, While you and I, dilly, dilly, Keep out of harm." Slowly he turned his head. He saw Addie and the kitten. The little girl sat on the bench beneath a huge oak tree. Eli's song caught in his throat.

There just beside the great tree and slightly behind Addie, was a lady in white. She was beautiful. Eli could clearly see the dark hair, which was gathered up on top of her head. He could see the arms she held out to the child. Yet there was something about her, an airy quality as if she could float away at any time.

"Addie's mother." The Graveyard Girl reached Eli, and she whispered to him. "Do you believe now?"

He could not speak. Nor could he turn away from the strange picture before him. He wanted to look away. There was love in every inch of the white figure. Eli could feel the weight of the devotion that had pulled her back from the other side.

He felt his heart break with longing. Where was his mother? Why did she not come to him? "She comes. Addie's mother comes. Yet my ma doesn't." He had not intended to say the words aloud.

"Oh, Eli, don't you understand?"

Rage swept through the boy, and he sprang to his feet. "I don't understand nothing but that I'm hanging around the wrong place."

He whirled to walk away, but she caught the sleeve of his shirt. "Wait, Eli. I came out here to tell you."

"Tell me what?" he demanded, but he was looking at her now. Looking at her red face and watery eyes, he knew with a terrible certainty.

"I'm sick," she said simply. "Maybe coming down with the fever." She drew a deep breath. "There are things you'll have to do."

His heart pounded against the wall of his chest, and his whole body began to shake. "No. No. I won't see you die. I won't take care of Addie, and won't watch you die." He was surprised to realize the shrieking voice bouncing against his ears belonged to him, but he kept talking. "I've had enough, done what I can. Do you hear me? I can't do it again. I can't."

Without waiting for a response, he swung his

body toward the cemetery entrance and began to walk. Run! the voice inside his head screamed. Run before they catch you! But his legs trembled too much for running.

At one grave he paused. There was an angel statue on the stone, and Eli reached out momentarily to touch the heavenly being's foot. "Lucky you are to be made of stone," he whispered. "I was like that once. Going to be that way again. Going to be stone same as you." He moved on toward the white picket gate.

Nine

ELI WALKED SLOWLY AWAY FROM ELMWOOD CEME-
tery, forcing his heavy legs and feet to move out
through the gate and down the abandoned streets,
not caring where he went, refusing to think, to
consider the fate of the Graveyard Girl or of little
Addie.

After several empty blocks, he let a thought
form. Go west, he told himself. No use just wandering around. Start walking west. Thinking was
hard, and he could not concentrate and make his
feet work at the same time. He stopped and leaned
against a brick building, closing his eyes.

When he opened them, Addie stood there,
waiting with her head down and her hand twisting
at a blond curl. "You've sneaked around and followed after me," he said softly, too weary to
shout.

She nodded. " 'Cause I had to. The Graveyard

Girl's sick. You have to take care of me." She did not look up at him, and her voice sounded frightened.

"You won't get no sympathy from me." He shook his head. "You've got your mother. I saw her."

Addie took a step toward him. "Mama can't stay with me. She doesn't have much longer."

"I can't stay neither. Go on back to the cemetery. Somebody there's bound to help you." He turned away from her.

"They'd put me in an asylum. Please, I want to stay at my house."

Anger gave him energy. "Look," he yelled. "I don't care one little whit what you're wanting. I don't care what you do, but you can't tag after me. Don't know why you'd want to." He shrugged his shoulders. "I'm just like my da. Can't count on me."

"No." Soft little sobs made her shoulders move. "You got to see to me."

Eli closed his eyes again and leaned his head back against the brick wall. Addie said nothing, but he could hear her sniffling. He couldn't just leave her crying in the street.

You're right, he thought. I do have to see to you. I'll see you locked up in St. Mary's orphan asylum. You won't be trailing after me like some stray dog then. He opened his eyes, took a deep breath, and straightened his body. "Come on," he said, and she skipped after him, happy, not even asking where they were headed.

At the deserted intersection, the boy paused. The Episcopal church that sponsored the home for children was, he thought, downtown, maybe not far from St. Peter's. He scratched his head. Too bad he hadn't asked the Graveyard Girl. Hadn't she mentioned going to St. Mary's School for Young Ladies? He bit his lip. Would she ever go back to school? If she really did have the fever, odds were not very good.

Eli gave himself a little shake. He would not think of Grace the Graveyard Girl now. He would not remember how excited she had become when she spoke of wanting to live. He would not remember how her gray eyes had sparkled.

Addie pulled at his arms. "What are you doing? Why are we just standing?"

"Directions. I'm studying on which way to go." A wagon loaded with black militia men was coming toward them, and Eli waved his hand at the driver who pulled his horses to a stop. "Stay right here," Eli instructed the little girl. "Don't you move. I got to talk to the man."

Keeping his eyes on the child, he walked the few feet to the head of the wagon. "Can you direct me on how to get to St. Mary's orphan asylum?"

"You needing a place to stay?" the driver asked.

"The little girl." Eli bent his head in Addie's direction. "Lost her folks to fever."

The man made a sympathetic clucking sound with his tongue. "We're headed to our camp. Go right by St. Mary's. Might as well to hop on back."

"I'm obliged to you. Much obliged." Eli motioned for Addie to come to him. "We're getting a ride," he said as he lifted her to the back of the wagon.

"A ride to where?" she demanded when they were settled and the wagon was moving again.

"Shush." He put his finger to his lips and frowned.

Addie was determined to talk. She turned to the man nearest her in the wagon. "Are you a soldier?" She pointed at the gun that lay across his lap.

"We keep the peace, miss."

"A piece of what? Can I see it?" Addie leaned around the man for a better look. Eli groaned and jerked at her hand, but she ignored him.

"We try to keep people from stealing and such as that, hand out the food rations down to the square."

"Well, that's very nice of you," said Addie as if her approval would mean a great deal.

For a time they rode quietly. Then the wagon stopped. "Orphan asylum's just over yonder round that corner," called the driver.

Eli gritted his teeth and jumped down. Addie, he was sure, knew now what he had in mind. She said nothing, letting him help her from the wagon, but she kept her eyes down, not looking at him.

Eli waved his hand at the driver and then turned back to Addie. She was not there. For a minute he was stumped. Then he caught sight of something, a bit of pink, Addie's dress. She was hiding behind a tree a few feet away.

Let her go, he told himself, you tried. When she gets hungry or sleepy, likely she'll find someone to help her.

He smiled and looked down at his hand, remembering how the brooch had felt in his palm. There was nothing to stop him from taking it now, nothing to stop him from leaving the stinking city.

For five determined steps, his resolve lasted, but as his foot hit the wooden street for the sixth time, his mother's face came to his mind. Her eyes held a disappointed look.

Eli whirled back. "Addie," he called, his voice full of exasperation, "come on out here else I'll come over there and get you out."

No sound came from behind the tree. Eli

stomped his foot. "Get over here, I say. You want me to just walk off and leave you?" No response.

He moved to the tree, put his hand on the big trunk, and reached around to grab Addie, but she was not there. He swung about, looking. There was no one, only buildings, empty and boarded up.

Not far away a cannon sounded, and the ground beneath Eli's feet vibrated with the sound. Where was Addie? Suddenly he felt as if he had lost Molly and would have to go home and confess to his ma.

He twisted about, his hand shading his eyes as he looked in each direction. He would still go out West, but before he could go, he would have to fulfill his responsibility to the little girl.

At first he ran down the board street, the sound of his feet echoing in his ears. He kept his head turning from side to side, his eyes searching for a blond curl or a piece of pink cloth.

Finally out of breath, he stopped. His stomach was balled into a painful knot, and his eyes stung from the smoke of the cannon. His mind was still trying to catch up to what had happened. A minute ago she had been there beside him, and then in an instant she was gone. Guess now she knows I'm not going to be her brother. Guess she finally believes I'm leaving. The noise of the cannon, the confusion, the stench of sewers and of death in the decaying city rose against Eli like a great black wall.

He clenched his fists and raised his face toward the tops of the buildings, a scream tearing its way out of his throat. "Molly!" he yelled. He had meant to yell Addie, and the sound of his sister's name startled him as it echoed back from the brick buildings.

As Eli stood there, sweat covered him like a thin coat of oil. The cannon boomed again, rattling the glass in the windows, and the sound propelled Eli with it down the streets once more, but this time it was Addie's name he yelled as he ran. "Addie, oh Addie," he said over and over. "Addie, where are you?"

He rounded a corner, and a hot gust of wind hit him full in the face. A small brick-and-wood building was on fire. The roof had already fallen into the center of the structure, and flames were eating their way around the windows. Eli watched, and one of the large glass windows burst outward from the heat. He began backing away, eyeing the other window, as yet undamaged. What he saw there made him suck in his breath sharply. It was the Grim Reaper, staring out of the fire, grinning his white bony grin directly at Eli. It was a poster advertising an elixir to guard against the yellow death. The building had been a medicine shop. To Eli it seemed that the face on the poster was drawing him into the fire, pulling him closer and closer into a shimmering red dance of death. When the window exploded, he jumped backward.

"Look out!" The warning was accompanied by a clattering sound, and Eli felt something push hard against him, knocking the wind from his chest. He found himself lying on the ground, a black face looming over him. McLemore! It was McLemore, and Eli jumped up, brushing himself off. He clutched at the man's sleeve. "You got to help me, McLemore," he pleaded. The dead wagon that had almost run him down was standing a few feet away, and Eli began pulling the man toward it. "You got to help me find her. You got to."

"Whoa! Who I got to find, boy? Just you slow down a mite. I almost run you down, you in such a hurry." McLemore reached into the wagon and pulled a water flask from under the seat. He unscrewed the top and handed it to Eli. "Here now, you take a drink of this here water first, then you tell me who it is we got to find."

Eli took the flask and sucked at it greedily. He hadn't realized he was so thirsty. When he finished, he wiped his mouth on the back of his hand, climbed up beside McLemore, and began to tell about Addie.

"Where you speck she might go to?"

McLemore flicked the leather strap against the horses' flanks and the wagon creaked forward.

Eli held his face in his hands, slumping in despair. "I don't know," he moaned through his fingers.

"Well, sir, let's us just think about this here thing for a minute." The wagon stopped as McLemore pulled back on the reins. He turned to face Eli. "Don't spose she took herself to her mama's house?"

It made sense. Addie would go home and wait for her mother to tell her what to do.

He nodded his head. "That's it. I sure do think that's it. Can you take me, McLemore? Can you take me to Carlile House?"

"Well . . ." McLemore turned to look at the boxes in the back of the wagon. "Don't speck any of them folks cares one way or the other." He frowned slightly. "The Graveyard Girl, though, I sure don't want nothing to upset Miss Grace."

Eli could not look at the man. McLemore did not know that Grace was sick, and Eli opened his mouth to tell him. But the words wouldn't come out. Eli could not say that the Graveyard Girl might have the fever. Maybe she doesn't, he told himself. Maybe she was just feeling puny this morning. Maybe she's better now. "Miss Grace is fond of Addie, right smart fond," he said, and he knew what he said was true.

McLemore seemed satisfied. "Get up," he called, and the great horses began to move. As the dead wagon creaked and groaned its way through the streets, Eli sat silently beside the man, watching the agony of Memphis. The few people who were out and about walked quickly, eyes down, as if they thought they could escape death by refusing to look it in the eye. Here and there were piles of charred rubble where buildings had been. Some still had curls of smoke rising from them. Occasionally, the cannon would boom, and McLemore would have to hold the reins tighter to keep the horses from bolting.

As they neared the street where Addie had lived, Eli watched as two shabbily dressed men struggled down the steps of a large white house. They were trying to carry an ornately carved table and were swearing at each other. Eli thought they were probably stealing the table. They didn't look the sort to live in a house like that.

He started to call out to McLemore, to tell him to stop the wagon, that a robbery was being committed, but he stayed quiet. There was no time to worry about tables now. Besides, the people who owned the table were probably dead anyway. The city was dying too. Nothing made sense anymore.

Eli jumped down as soon as they stopped in

front of the big white house. "You can go on now," he called up to McLemore.

McLemore frowned. "Don't know. I don't cotton to the idea of that little girl being all alone out there." He waved his arm toward the city. "Still, where else could you look? Anyways, I speck I can spare the time to see is the little one here." He began to climb down from the wagon.

Addie wasn't there. Eli and McLemore searched through the empty house and yard, even looking under the big back porch, but the little girl was nowhere to be found.

In the garden Eli paused for a quick look at the rosebush, guilt making his face red. When McLemore's gone, are you going to dig up the treasure? He had no time to answer his own question because another demanded his attention. When you find Addie, are you going to take her back to the orphans' asylum? Are you going to hold her arm and drag her off to live with strangers?

"Let's go, boy. The child's not here." McLemore's hand was on Eli's shoulder, guiding him down the walk toward the wagon. Eli was suddenly very tired and let himself be led away from the house.

They had already started to climb back into the wagon when the feeling came over Eli, making him pause. "Wait, McLemore," he shouted. "I have to go back in there." The feeling was coming even stronger now. Eli turned and raced back to the house. He half expected to see Addie standing in the doorway, but it was empty.

Something was there, though, something that pulled Eli through the door and down the hallway to the room that had been Addie's mother's.

When he entered that room, the feeling came so strongly that it was as if it was flooding into his own body, becoming a part of him. He stood there waiting for something more, but the room was as empty as the rest of the house. Only Eli and the feeling were there. He heard McLemore's footsteps coming up the front steps. "Hurry," said Eli suddenly. "Whatever you want. Hurry."

It wasn't a voice really, at least not one that anyone could hear. It was just there all at once inside Eli's head.

"Pinchgut," the feeling said. "The river near your house."

Ten

ELI ALMOST COLLIDED WITH MCLEMORE AS HE turned and raced out of the house. "Pinchgut!" he yelled over his shoulder. "She's in Pinchgut."

He was already on the wagon seat by the time the man got back to him. Eli had picked up the reins, and he handed them over to McLemore. "Hurry!" he urged.

The driver cocked his eyebrow. "What makes you to figure she's at Pinchgut? Why she go down to that place?"

"I don't know," answered Eli. He shrugged his shoulders. "Just a feeling I have. That's all, but it's a powerful strong feeling."

McLemore snorted. "Some feeling, Pinchgut," he muttered under his breath. "Sweet little girl like that Addie got no business in a place like Pinchgut."

They were through the main part of the city,

heading down the hill into Pinchgut when the answer came to Eli.

"Addie's da has a warehouse down by the river." He turned to face McLemore. "Remember, she talked about it this morning."

"Could be," said the man. "Could be she might go there."

But when they reached the great brick building, the door was chained and padlocked. Every window was covered with heavy planks. Eli and McLemore walked around the building several times looking for a spot large enough for a small girl to crawl into.

"Even a little old mouse ain't getting in that place." McLemore eyed Eli. "What now?"

"Don't know." Disappointment showed plainly on Eli's face. "I'm stumped."

McLemore took a deep breath. "Well, I got to get on my way." His voice was apologetic. "Folks is counting on me." He climbed back into the wagon. "I'll give you a ride back you want one."

"Reckon I'll keep looking, thanks."

"I figured." He flicked the reins over the horses. "I'll come back later, I get time."

"Thanks to you!" Eli called as the wagon rumbled away.

There was still no Addie, but Eli felt comforted somehow by the familiar surroundings of Pinchgut. He made one last circle around the warehouse, planning to follow the street from there down to the river, but he was pulled instead the other way. He knew, without really planning it, that he was going to his old house. If he could just be there for a while, surrounded by the things he had known before the world collapsed around him, maybe, just maybe he could figure the whole thing out. Maybe he would know where to look next. Maybe he would know what to do with Addie when he found her.

There were remains of burned mattresses and bedding in the yard. Eli studied the charred pile from a distance for just a minute. Someone had been in the house since he left. Slowly he moved toward the door.

"What y'all want?" Eli was standing on his own front stoop, and the voice came at him from the open window. When his eyes adjusted to the shadows, he saw that the words were coming from a boy a little younger than he was. He wore an old shirt that Eli had left behind.

"This is my house," Eli stammered. "Who are you?"

"Jefferson!" a voice called from inside. "Who's out there?"

"Don't know, Mama. He ain't said yet. Claims it's his house though."

Another head appeared behind that of the boy.

"Well, anyway it used to be my house." Eli

backed halfway off the stoop. He didn't want any trouble from these people. "I just wanted to see it again. That's all."

The door opened, and a woman with a thin, tired face stood there.

"Tell me your name, child." The woman waited for Eli's answer, her arms folded across her chest.

Suddenly Eli grew defiant. "It's Eli," he almost yelled. "Eli Mahoney."

The woman moved over and motioned Eli inside. "Could be you're right about this house being yours," she said. "I heard of you folks."

"Mama," the boy complained, "we ain't going to just go easy. How we know he ain't lying? What we going to do? We fixing to be living in the street again? Probably even say I got to take off this shirt."

"Jefferson," his mother said, "right is right!" The woman hurried around the room, picked up a few pots, and started throwing them in a wooden crate. "Won't take long to gather," she said. "Didn't bring much, won't take much."

Eli saw the sad look on the woman's face.

"Son, you take off this boy's shirt," she commanded the boy.

"No!" Eli said suddenly.

The woman and her son turned to look at him. He shrugged his shoulders. "You can keep the shirt, and you're welcome to it." They were both staring at him, waiting. "Keep the house too," he added.

The woman smiled. "Where's your folks? They run from the fever? Or if you got you a new place my Joe'll carry your things to it when he gets back. Him and Jefferson, they'll help you even if it's all the way to the other side of town."

Eli shook his head. "Everyone's dead," he said. "My ma and my little sister." He looked around at the table, the stove, and at his mother's sewing basket still in the corner. "I thought it would help me to see her things. I thought could I see my ma's things maybe she'd sort of come back to me, tell me what to do."

The woman was nodding her head sympathetically. "You want to stay here you can. You got a right."

"I got things to do," Eli said. "I got someone to hunt, but I'm sure enough grateful for the offer." He turned to leave. "My ma ain't here," he whispered. "She ain't here to tell me what to do."

The woman had leaned forward to catch his words. "You wondering what your mama'd want you to do? Why, boy, don't you already know? She'd tell you to do right, child. Us mamas, we always want our boys to do right."

It was the truth, and Eli knew it. Standing there looking at this other boy's mother, he knew it. His mother would want him to do right, would demand it, just as Jefferson's mother had demanded it of her son. It was right for him to find Addie. It was right for him to stay with her and to protect her. It was right, too, for him to go back to Elmwood. When he found Addie, he would go back to the cemetery. He would go back to see the Graveyard Girl. "God," he prayed. "Let her be alive. Let her live." And it felt right to pray.

Outside, he turned away from the bluff and started walking in the direction that would take him out of the slums. Addie hadn't been at her father's warehouse. Maybe he had imagined that inner voice telling him to search Pinchgut, but it came again, this time more than a feeling.

"Along the river."

The words jerked at him. "What?" Eli spun around. "Who's there?" His voice echoed along the empty street. "Who said that?" he cried. "Where are you?"

There was no one near him. At the end of the street he could see a buggy stop in front of a shanty. A stoop-shouldered man who was probably a doctor got out and carried a black bag toward the door, but he was too far away to have called to Eli. A hungry-looking dog slinked around the corner of a nearby hovel, but there was no human close by.

The voice came again. "Along the river, along

the river," it was saying. "My little girl's along the river!"

Eli shook his head as if to clear it. "I hear you," he said. "I'll go now."

At the water's edge, he stood panting and listening. "Now what?" he asked, but no answer came. He tried to calm himself by breathing deep of the air off the river. It was good air after the stench of the city, but Eli was too tense to notice.

He looked about him. Here on the riverfront the close-packed, squalid shacks of Pinchgut gave way to wide cobbled landings leading to docks and warehouses, but the emptiness of it all made him uneasy. Like the rest of the city, everything on the wharf had changed. Eli's ears should have been filled with shouts of sweating men, but nothing came to him except the beating of the waves against the river's bank.

What should he do? His body ached, and he considered resting for a minute, maybe even dipping his hands and feet into the water, but he was afraid to sit down. Better to be up, to keep moving.

For a considerable time, he walked aimlessly. Leaving the cobbled streets, he made his way along the muddy marshes at the edge of the river. The sound of the waves was louder there, and Eli saw that the water was rushing by faster than usual.

He had not noticed as he walked how much

distance he had put between himself and the city, and was surprised to find, when he turned to look, that even the tallest buildings had disappeared from his sight.

Maybe he should turn back. He paused, considering, but then the quiet was disturbed by a noise behind him. He swung around toward the river in time to see a small poplar tree that had clung to the bank slowly slip into the water.

He realized with a start that the water had risen considerably. There must have been heavy rain somewhere up the river just like in Memphis. The sight of the small tree, now slipping into the current and being carried swiftly down the river, sent a chill down Eli's spine. The feeling was back inside him. Addie was near this racing water. He knew it.

He began to run. "Addie!" he yelled over the rush of the water. "Addie, where are you?"

Then he saw her. She stood on a small hill several yards away. The wind was lifting her golden curls, and she was looking at Eli. He waved his arms. "Addie, wait for me."

"No!" she shouted. "No, you're not my friend anymore." She whirled around and, running, disappeared over the rise.

I'll catch her, Eli told himself, she can't outrun me. But a cold warning inside whispered a doubt.

The mud caught at his feet, but he plowed on, stopping suddenly at the top of the hill.

A dilapidated boathouse perched on an old dock, the water beating relentlessly at the piling beneath the pier. As Eli watched, the structure bent under the force of the mighty river. "Addie," he yelled. "Are you in that boat shed? If you are, come out quick."

No sound came to him except the pounding of the water against the bank and against the old pier. From his spot near the dock, Eli surveyed the area. Just upriver from the boathouse, a small skiff rested on the bank. Thank the Lord, he thought, she didn't take it into her foolish head to put off down the river. No, she ain't that desperate to get away from me.

The grass along the river was short, and Eli could see for some distance. There was no place else. Addie had to be in the boathouse. If she didn't come out at once, he would have to go in to get her. Eli saw the dock bend with the water's pressure and sway sickeningly. He did not want to go in. "Addie," he pleaded, "I know you're in there, and you got to come out. Listen to me. I'm sorry about the orphans' asylum. Powerful sorry, but I decided now that I want to stay with you. Sure enough, I promise."

No answer came. Eli bowed his neck and moved toward the tilting dock. "Easy," he whispered. "Walk easy," and he held his breath as he put a foot on the old wood. There were cracks in the planks. Just once he looked down at the swirling river, then turned his gaze back to the shed.

The door, when he pressed against it, did not open. Had she locked it somehow from inside? "Addie," he begged. "Open up." He was afraid to pound, afraid to do anything that might shake the dock, but when he tried the door again it moved slightly.

When the opening was wide enough, he took a deep breath and eased into the dark building. For a moment he couldn't see, but his eyes adjusted. An old bench stood by one wall, and some fishing poles hung on another. There was nothing else. No Addie.

You've lost her again, he accused himself, but the thought was brief because all at once Eli was fighting for his balance as the floor of the boat shed lurched beneath his feet. He was falling, falling amid the wood and tin of the boathouse, falling toward the raging water. A piece of roof struck him hard on the back, but he ignored the pain.

He had to grab, had to grab something that would hold him. For a fraction of a second, he thought there was nothing, and a terrible cry tore from his throat. Then one of his flailing arms hit wood, part of what had once been the boathouse floor. The board was still fastened to part of the piling left standing.

Eli latched on to the plank, wrapping both arms around it. For at least a minute he would be safe, but he dangled above the water. How long would the timber hold?

Gradually he became aware of screaming, and he looked frantically about him. Addie stood in the skiff, and he realized she had been there all along, flattened against the bottom, out of sight.

"Eli," she shrieked. "Oh, Eli!"

There was only one chance. "Listen," he yelled. "You got to listen to me. Get out of the boat. Push hard till you get it in the river. The current will carry it my way. When it's close I'll drop. Maybe I can grab hold."

"I'm scared, Eli! I'm scared you'll get drowned."

"Do it, Addie. Push the boat! Whatever happens you go back to town. Find someone and ask them to take care of you."

Addie made no move. "Now!" Eli yelled. "Get out now and push that boat!"

She did. The boat was small, but so was Addie. Eli watched her bend and heave. Inch by inch she pushed the skiff, and all the while Eli's board swayed up and down, threatening to break. "Hurry!" he screamed.

Finally, Addie had the boat at the water's

edge. "Good job," he yelled. "Now one more push, then get back away from the water!" The thought flashed through his mind that if he drowned, Addie would have to watch.

So intently was he staring toward the front of the boat that for a second he did not realize what the child was doing, but then he saw her. "No," he screamed. "No, Addie, don't get in that boat!"

It was too late. With a lunge Addie tumbled in, and the skiff careened downriver toward Eli.

Now two lives were at risk, but he couldn't spend time on that thought. Eli had to put his energy into getting to that boat. The water was fast. He took one deep breath, and the boat made great progress. Then it was close, very close. Turn loose, he told himself. You got to turn loose. For one instant he felt himself falling, then water, cold, strong water.

The skiff was not near enough for him to touch. He fought to stay up, but he knew he couldn't last long. Something was flying through the air! A rope! Addie had found the rope someone had used for tying the boat. One end was fastened to the bow, and Addie had flung the other out toward Eli. He hurtled himself through the rushing water, and his hand fastened on the rope. For a second he was pulled under. He came back to the surface sputtering and coughing brown water.

"Hang on, Eli," Addie called. "Please hang on."

Fighting the river, he worked hand over hand until at last he could grasp the edge of the skiff. "I'll help you," Addie said, and amazingly it was her little arms that pulled him over.

He tumbled in and lay panting on the bottom of the boat. "My Eli," said the little girl, and she patted him over and over on his wet head.

It was a long time before he could move or talk. Feeling the river toss the small boat, he knew they were still in danger, but no strength was left in him. Finally he pulled himself to a sitting position. Addie was staring at him, her eyes big and round. "Why'd you get in?" he demanded. "We might drown yet."

"I wanted to be with you, Eli," she whispered. "You said we could stay together, and I wanted to be with you."

"Well," he said, "it's powerful lucky for me you did. Saved my life, that's what you done."

She smiled. "Where are we going now?" He could see that she had no fear, that she trusted him completely.

"Don't know," he said. He breathed deeply, trying to calm his racing heart. "Well, we're both safe for now at least." He stretched out his arm and stuck his fingers into the fast current. "We ain't got nothing to use for an oar, nothing to fight this rush with. Might just float plumb to New Orleans, Louisiana."

Addie yawned and arranged herself to lie down in the bottom of the boat. "Maybe my mama can watch over us." A tear slipped out one eye and down her cheek. "She won't be back to talk, though. My mama had to say good-bye."

Eli swallowed hard. "I'll take care of you, Addie." Once the words were said they sounded right in his ears. "I'll stay with you as long as you need me."

She smiled. "I'm glad, Eli," she said simply. "I'm awful glad you didn't get dead." She closed her eyes then.

Eli watched Addie sleep and marveled that she could do so in a tiny boat on the angry river. The side of the boat was rough against his back as he leaned against it. They were away from the city completely now. Only willows and tall grass decorated the muddy sides of the great stream.

"River," he said, "where you taking us?" He stared so long at the bank that the trees, grass, and water began to blur before his eyes, and at first he thought he might be seeing things.

He sat up straight and rubbed his eyes. No, it was true. The land was not as far away as it had once been. The current was still carrying the boat quickly downstream, but as the boat raced, it also moved gradually closer to the east bank.

"Wake up." He reached out to shake Addie. "Wake up. We got to be ready." He knew when he saw the big willow that the current would carry the boat near enough to the tree, and when it did, they would be ready. Eli crouched, his muscles tense, then with a yell he sprang upward.

Grabbing a branch, he pulled it down and steadied the boat with his feet while Addie scrambled out. Then he swung himself up and over, landing in the oozy mud. The current took the boat bobbing on down the Mississippi.

"Might be somebody else will use it 'fore it sees Orleans," Eli told Addie, as he bent at the water's edge to wash. When he rose, he took her hand. "We got us some walking to do, Puddin'," he said, "and the sun's not far from setting."

They moved without talking, keeping near the river as a guide. The sound of the water was a comfort to Eli, and Addie too seemed soothed, not complaining about the weeds or the mud. Her steps were slower and slower, though, and Eli knew they would not be in the city by nightfall.

"That might be our best bet for a dry bed," he told the girl when they spotted an abandoned wagon off in the weeds. "We'll be back in Memphis early morning, get us a breakfast handout from the militia in the square, and a ride to Elmwood."

"Do you think she's bad? Do you think Grace's bad sick with the fever?"

They were at the wagon now, and Eli rested against the rickety wheel for a second before he answered. "I don't know. Maybe not." He shrugged his shoulders, mystified. "Something's been on our side lately. Something mighty powerful."

Addie was asleep almost as soon as she lay down, but Eli sat up, watching the moonlight play on the water and listening to its mighty rush. "I should've never said I hated you, River," he whispered. "We fought today, you and me. You're a terrible enemy, but you helped us too, I reckon. You run inside me, River. Guess you always will." He shook his head. "Forget California."

When the September night grew cool, he gathered the straw from the end of the wagon and covered Addie with it. Then he too lay down and fell asleep listening to the river and praying for the Graveyard Girl.

Eleven

ELMWOOD CEMETERY, WHEN THEY REACHED IT THE next morning, was different. Workers still lifted shovels of brown dirt dug from the long lines of graves. The great wagon still stood in the same spot waiting with its load of coffins. The dove in the hydrangea bush still held forth with its same mournful call, but Elmwood Cemetery was different.

"The bell," Eli told Addie. "The bell ought to be ringing." A tightness grew around his heart. He took the little girl's hand to hurry her, and it was hard not to hold his breath. "We'll know when we see the cottage door," he said, and he walked as fast as she could follow.

"Oh!" Addie stopped and pointed. Eli saw it too. On the door was the yellow sign, the terrible signal of fever.

He leaned against the trunk of an elm tree and

took a deep breath. "Go see if you can find your kitten," he said.

"You won't go off and leave me?"

"No, now, I've done promised. Cross my heart, I'll stay with you least till your aunt comes. Run on. I've got to see about the Graveyard Girl."

"Will she die?" Addie's lip was quivering.

"I hope not. I sure do hope not."

McLemore sat on the cottage step. His huge shoulders sagged, and Eli noticed for the first time the deep lines in his face. "She's bad. Even Miss Grace's ain't safe from the yellow jack." The black man dropped his eyes, expecting no reply, and there was none for Eli to offer.

The door was open to catch the breeze. When Eli put his foot on the step, he could see the Graveyard Girl's bed, and he recognized the form of Nurse Tyler as she bent over the patient.

He knocked. "I'm a friend of Miss Grace's," he said. "Can I come in just a bit?"

"Yes," whispered the Graveyard Girl. "Yes, I want to talk to Eli."

Miss Tyler was between the boy and the bed, and Eli leaned around her to see Grace. Her skin was yellow, the horrible, familiar yellow. She was looking at Eli. Her gray eyes were watery, but still, they held him in the same steady gaze.

She knows things, Eli thought. She knows why my ma never comes to me.

The nurse turned to him. "You've had the fever, right, boy?" She wiped the sweat from her face onto a large handkerchief.

"Yes."

"Well, come in then. I'll get me a breath of air." She put the lid back on a bottle of medicine before she ambled to the door.

"Addie?" the Graveyard Girl asked.

"She's all right. I'll stay with her. Addie's mother helped me. Her mother helped me find her."

"I want to hear about it."

"I'll tell you." He reached for a chair and pulled it close to the bed. "We'll have lots of time to talk when you're feeling better, but . . ." He paused and looked down. "I've got to ask you something."

"You want to ask me about your mother. You want me to tell you why your mother does not visit you, don't you?"

"Yes."

She smiled. "Oh, Eli, you know. You know why your mother doesn't come."

"No. No I don't. I want my ma. I want to see her so bad."

"But she's with you, isn't she? She's never really left. Don't you hear your mother's voice in your head? Don't you know what she would want you to do, always? You don't need a form or words to be said aloud. Your mother *is* with you, Eli."

He pushed back his chair, stood, and walked to the window where he could look out at his mother's grave. "Yes," he said. "She's fastened inside my head and heart. Even when I'm old, all gray and bent, my ma will be the same inside my head."

"It's a treasure, Eli. A very special treasure left you."

The truth of her words filled him. "Better than a diamond brooch," he said, and he came back to her bedside.

"What about your father?" she asked when he was settled. "What will you do when your father comes back? And he will come back. He's bound to."

He shook his head. "I'll have to study on it." He bit his lip. "I ran too, you know. Guess I understand my da some better now, but still . . ." His words trailed off, and he shrugged.

"Maybe you can forgive him someday."

"Maybe." He reached for the damp cloth and spread it on her forehead. "Please try to get well," he said. "Please try awful hard to get well."

"Oh, I will. I'll try." Her voice was low, and he had to lean close to hear. "But, Eli, this life is just the door. There's more, so much more still to come."

She closed her eyes. He watched the blanket over her body rise and fall as she breathed. She's still alive, he told himself. At least for now, she's still alive.

"I'll go now," he said. "I'll go ring the bell. Don't worry, I'll ring the bell until you're well."

He saw her smile.

Eli did ring the bell. He rang it while Grace was sick. He rang it when she died. He rang the bell, and he finally cried.

At last, in late October, the frost came, and in a few days the *Appeal* announced that the epidemic had been declared officially over. Celebrations and services of thanksgiving were held.

Eli and Addie watched as the city came back to life. Business, churches, and schools opened. Train depots were full of returning travelers, and the river was full of boats.

One day as Eli stood on the bluff, he looked down to see a group of roustabouts unloading furniture from a ship. One of them, a large man with red hair, was familiar, and Eli looked closer. "Da," he whispered. He watched for a long time, but he did not go down to the man. He would, he knew, someday. Someday he would go down to speak to his father, and someday they would fish again together.

Addie's aunt Elizabeth came by train from Charleston, South Carolina. She started at once to clean the house, and she hired servants to help her. "We'll get you in a school, boy," she said to Eli. "You're part of our family now."

He was glad to be part of a family, but the others would never be forgotten.

Frequently, as he walked down by the river, his sister Molly skipped beside him, chattering or singing a silly song. In the evenings when the sun began to go down, Eli could sometimes smell his mother's cooking and hear her call him to supper. And the Graveyard Girl would come to him, always, each time he heard the tolling of a bell.